Official Encyclopedia

Published in the United States by
THUNDER'S MOUTH PRESS
841 Broadway, Fourth Floor, New York, NY 10003

Published under license from Wizards of the Coast, Inc.

First published in 1999 by Carlton Books Limited,
20 St Anne's Court, Wardour Street, London, W1V 3AW

ISBN 156025 211 1

Printed and bound in Italy

Executive Editor: Tim Dedopulos
Project Editor: Roland Hall
Art Director: Zoe Mercer
Design: Adam Wright
Production: Bob Bhamra

ACKNOWLEDGEMENTS
Thanks to: The superlative Jesper Myrfors, Mike Elliott, Henry Stern, Mark Rosewater, Chaz Elliott, Hans Reifenrath, Melody Alder, the superhuman Eric Nancarrow, Richard Garfield, Bill Rose, Jonathan Tweet, Jan-Maree Madigan Bourgeois and Paul Bazakas.

Distributed by
Publishers Group West
1700 Fourth Street
Berkeley, CA 94710

Author
Beth Moursund started playing **Magic** in August 1993 and has been an active presence in the game ever since. Widely recognized for her **Magic** rules knowledge, Beth is a **Magic** Pro Tour judge for Wizards of the Coast. She writes for magazines including *The Duelist* and *InQuest*, and she wrote the *Magic The Gathering* Official Strategy Guide.

Official
Encyclopedia

The Complete Card Guide Volume 4

Beth Moursund

THUNDER'S
MOUTH
PRESS

Contents

How to Use This Guide

WHICH CARDS ARE INCLUDED

This **Magic: The Gathering**® card guide includes the most current version of every non-promotional **Magic** card that has been printed since the release of *Exodus*™, as well as the most significant of the promotional cards, and other interesting cards that have been produced, for one reason or another, throughout the last twelve months of the trading card game **Magic: The Gathering**.

For cards which have multiple versions in the same set, all versions of the card are shown. Many cards which originated in the basic set have undergone several revisions since their initial release; only the most current version of the card is shown. If a card was discontinued from the basic set, the most current version of that card can be found in a previous volume of the *Magic: The Gathering Official Encyclopedia*.

Limited-edition expansions are reproduced in their entirety, including cards that have been reprinted; the entry for each card indicates in which set the most current version of the card appears.

USING THE CARD CAPTIONS

All of the cards in the card guide section are accompanied by a caption. All but the promotional and misprint cards use the following format:

NAME

This line indicates the full, complete name of the card as printed on the card or corrected by errata. Cards for which there are multiple pieces of art within the same set are followed by a version number indicating which of the several functionally identical cards is referred to.

VERSIONS

This line lists all of the sets in which this card has been printed in functionally identical form, followed by the relative rarity of the card in that set (if applicable). These are listed in order from least to most recent version of the card. The sets are indicated with the following abbreviations:

The rarity of the cards is indicated with the following abbreviations:

C: The card is considered a common card; it appears on the common sheet.
U: The card is considered an uncommon card; it appears on the uncommon sheet.
R: The card is considered a rare card; it appears on the rare sheet.
L: The card is considered a land card; it appears on the land sheet. (Lands in *Chronicles* and some limited-edition expansions do not appear on the land sheet, and so are listed as common, uncommon, or rare. These land cards are still considered lands.)

A number following the letter indicates the number of times the card appears on the card sheet; for example, a U2 appears twice on the uncommon sheet. Cards with no number appear once on the sheet indicated.

Limited-edition Expansions:		*Basic Set:*
AN: *Arabian Nights*®	PO: *Portal*™	A: *Alpha*™ *Edition*
AQ: *Antiquities*®	SA: *Portal Second Age*™	B: *Beta*™ *Edition*
LG: *Legends*®	3K: *Portal Three Kindgoms*™	UL: *Unlimited*™ *Edition*
DK: *The Dark*®	CH: *Chronicles*™	RV: *Revised*™ *(Third Edition)*
FE: *Fallen Empires*™	TE: *Tempest*™	4E: *Fourth Edition*™
IA: *Ice Age*™	ST: *Stronghold*™	5E: *Fifth Edition*™
HM: *Homelands*™	EX: *Exodus*™	6E: *Classic*™ *(Sixth Edition*™*)*
AL: *Alliances*™	US: *Urza's Saga*™	6S: *Starter*™ *(Sixth Edition)*
MI: *Mirage*™	UL: *Urza's Legacy*™	
VI: *Visions*™	UD: *Urza's Destiny*™	
WE: *Weatherlight*™	UG: *Unglued*™	

An asterisk (*) following the set abbreviation indicates that this version of the card is functionally different from the previously listed version. (For a description of the functional changes in cards that have appeared in the basic set, including all cards that have been reprinted from expansions, see *The Pocket Player's Guide for **Magic: The Gathering**—Classic (Sixth Edition).*) For a description of the functional changes in cards reprinted in *Chronicles,* see *The Duelist,* issue #7, pages 100–101.)

CURRENT ERRATA

This lists any errata that applies to the most current version of the card. Sometimes, the entire revised card text is shown; when this has not been possible, only the affected portion of the card text is replaced, excerpted or referred to.

For expansion cards that have been reprinted in the basic set or *Chronicles,* any previous errata has been incorporated into the current version and so is not shown; instead, readers are referred to only the most current version of the card for current wording.

For example, consider the card Dark Ritual in Urza's Saga:

DARK RITUAL
Versions: **A, B, UL, RV, 4E, 5E, IA, MI, TE, US: C**
Current Errata: **none**

This card appeared in *Urza's Saga* as a common card. A functionally identical version of the card has been printed in many different editions as a common card.

Next is Shatter in the *Classic* section of the book:

SHATTER
Versions: **A, B, UL, RV, 4E, 5E, IA, TE, 6E: C**
Current Errata: none

The current wording of Shatter appears on the *Classic* card; no errata has since been issued to alter that wording.

The book contains the most current official information available at press time; however, new **Magic** cards and card rulings are being released all the time, which may modify or invalidate the information in this book. Any official errata issued on cards after June 1, 1999 supersedes any information presented here.

USING THE DECK-BUILDERS' INDEXES

Pages 151 through 172 contain the Deckbuilder's Indexes. These were specially created to enable easy deck planning and building by listing cards from a wide variety of different categories, and have been simplified in format from previous volumes of the encyclopedia for greater usability.

Each index entry has a description of the category. This is followed by a list of all cards from the *Sixth Edition* of the basic set and all expansions through *Urza's Legacy* that fall into that index category.

Every effort was made to include all of the cards under all of the pertinent categories; however, many categories, no matter how narrowly defined, are subject to interpretation, and so may be missing cards which might be thought to fall into that index (or even including some that wouldn't be thought to fall into that index). Therefore, these lists should certainly not be considered definitive for the purposes of interpreting card rulings or arbitrating game play.

A Visual Guide to Magic Cards

There have been thirty different English language sets, more than forty foreign releases, and dozens of speciality cards — it's hard to keep track of them all, and sometimes difficult to tell one from the other. The following guide, which describes and illustrates all **Magic** releases to date, is designed to help players and collectors distinguish between these different sets. All of the cards shown here are reproduced from the original cards at full size; therefore, they will vary in size and may vary slightly in color and legibility from the other card images in the book.

ALPHA

These cards (right) have black borders and are primarily distinguished by very rounded card corners. *Alpha* deck boxes lack a UPC bar code. *Alpha* (and *Beta*) booster packs are flat brown and are labeled **Magic: The Gathering**. The thirty-two-page *Alpha* rulebook has a picture of a Bog Wraith on the cover and contains "Worzel's Story" by Richard Garfield.

BETA

These cards (right) also have black borders and are primarily distinguished by their less-rounded card corners. (All cards printed since *Beta* have had these same corners.) Individual *Beta* deck boxes have a UPC bar code on the bottom (missing from the *Alpha* deck box). *Alpha* and *Beta* booster packs are identical. The forty-page *Beta* rulebook also has a Bog Wraith on the cover, but "Worzel's Story" was dropped in favor of a summary of play, an FAQ, and an index.

COLLECTORS' EDITION AND INTERNATIONAL COLLECTORS' EDITION

These cards (left) have black borders and are primarily distinguished by their square-cut corners and the gold border on the card back, which is labeled *Collectors' Edition*™ or *International Edition*. Each complete set is packaged in a single box labeled *Collectors' Edition* or *International Collectors' Edition*™.

UNLIMITED

These cards (right) have white borders and can be distinguished from other white-bordered editions by the presence of an illustrated "beveled" edge and, like *Revised,* a copyright on the bottom of the card attributing the card art to the artist. The deck boxes and booster packs have the words *"Unlimited Edition"* on them. The *Unlimited* rulebook is identical to the *Beta* rulebook.

REVISED

These cards (right) have white borders and can be distinguished from other white-bordered editions by the absence of the illustrated "beveled" edge on the card. Also, a change in the films in this printing caused many *Revised* cards to look lighter or faded compared to *Unlimited, Fourth, Fifth* and *Classic Edition* cards. The deck boxes and booster packs are labeled *"Revised Edition."* The *Revised* rulebook has a Shivan Dragon on the cover.

FOURTH AND FIFTH EDITION

These cards (left) have white borders and can be distinguished by the presence of both the illustrated "beveled" edge on the card and a Wizards of the Coast copyright at the bottom of the card (1997 for *Fifth* and 1995 for *Fourth*). Also, *Fourth* was the first set to incorporate the ⊤.

The deck boxes and booster packs are labeled *Fourth* or *Fifth Edition*. Starter decks for both sets display the five mana symbols, and the foil boosters feature one of five pieces of art from the appropriate set. The *Fourth Edition* rulebook was the first to have a color cover.

CLASSIC (SIXTH) EDITION

These (right) are white-bordered, with the "beveled" edge, and can be identified by their expansion symbol, a VI, appearing in the lower right corner below the art. The copyright notice (1999) and art credit are also centered at the bottom of the card.

LIMITED-EDITION EXPANSIONS AND PROMOTIONAL CARDS

These cards (left) are black-bordered and can be identified as belonging to a particular expansion by the expansion symbol which appears below the lower right corner of the art.

The expansion symbols for the existing limited-edition expansions are:

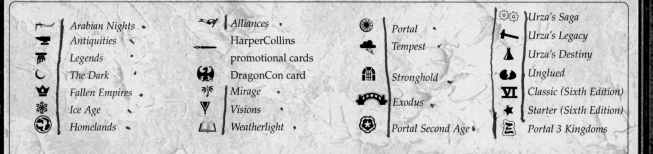

Arabian Nights	Alliances	Portal	Urza's Saga
Antiquities	HarperCollins promotional cards	Tempest	Urza's Legacy
Legends			Urza's Destiny
The Dark	DragonCon card	Stronghold	Unglued
Fallen Empires	Mirage	Exodus	Classic (Sixth Edition)
Ice Age	Visions		Starter (Sixth Edition)
Homelands	Weatherlight	Portal Second Age	Portal 3 Kingdoms

UNLIMITED-EDITION EXPANSIONS

Chronicles cards (above) are white-bordered and can be distinguished from other white-bordered cards by the expansion symbol indicating the original expansion the card appeared in; this appears below the lower-right corner of the art.

FOREIGN EDITIONS

Most **Magic** sets from *Legends* on have been released in at least one foreign language; in some cases multiple editions of the set have been released in translation, as have special card sets only available in particular languages. In general, these cards (above) can be distinguished by the card faces and packaging, which are translated into the corresponding language; the back of the cards is the original English card back.

COMMEMORATIVE COLLECTOR'S EDITION DECK SETS

These cards (right) have gold borders and rounded corners, with an appropriate legend and logo on the back. Cards can be identified as belonging to a particular deck from that *Collector Set* by the gold signature of that deck's creator, which appears near the lower right corner of the art. The back of the cards tells which deck set the card is from: for the illustrated example to the right, the **Magic: The Gathering** Pro Tour™ logo and "Inaugural Tournament New York City February 1996" legend show that the card is from the Pro Tour Collector Set—Inaugural Edition.

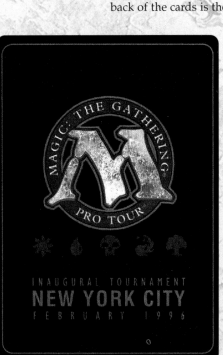

OVERVIEW

The fourth **Magic**® "stand-alone expansion," the *Urza's Saga*™ set pioneered a new format. Instead of the 60-card randomized decks of its predecessors, it featured 75-card "tournament packs." These were designed to make it easier to run Sealed-Deck tournaments.

The set introduced two new card mechanics: "echo" and "cycling."

Echo is solely a creature ability. It allows you to play a creature on an installment plan: pay half now and half next turn. If you don't pay, the creature is sacrificed. Echo also serves as a defense against creature-stealing spells and abilities, as each change of control resets the echo payment. An opponent who doesn't have the same color mana as you can't keep the creature, since he or she can't pay the echo cost.

Cycling can appear on any card type—the set even includes five lands (one for each color) with cycling. For two mana, you can discard a card with cycling and draw a replacement. This allows more flexibility in deck construction, as you can include cycling cards that are only useful in limited circumstances but are extremely powerful at the right time. If you draw one when it's not needed, you can "cycle" it and draw something else.

The *Urza's Saga* set also introduced three new groups of enchantments. "Sleeping" enchantments come into play as do-nothing enchantments,

but when some triggering event occurs, they change to creatures. "Growing" enchantments (foreshadowed by the *Tempest*™ card Legacy's Allure) add a counter each turn, growing in power until they're eventually sacrificed to produce an effect. And "perpetual" enchantments return to their owner's hand when they go to a graveyard from play.

THE STORY

The *Urza's Saga* set covers the longest span of any **Magic** expansion story to date. It begins during the last part of the Brothers' War (overlapping with the *Antiquities*® expansion) and chronicles the travels of Urza over the next four thousand years. At the time of the Brothers' War, Urza was a powerful artificer but not yet a planeswalker. The final battle of the war was fought in the forest of Argoth. The cataclysm as Urza and Mishra set their full forces against each other not only destroyed the forest—it also shattered the entire continent of Terisiare and set the plane of Dominia adrift in the Multiverse. So much power was released that Urza transcended mortality, becoming a planeswalker.

Urza blamed the lords of Phyrexia for corrupting his brother and causing the disaster. Realizing his new powers as a planeswalker, he dedicated himself to destroying them. He teamed up with a renegade Phyrexian named Xantcha, who

showed him the way to Phyrexia; however, he was not nearly powerful enough to beat the Phyrexians in their own territory and barely escaped with his life. Fleeing, he and Xantcha found their way to the plane of Serra, home of the Serra angels and a sisterhood of human warrior-priestesses. There, they were healed and learned more of the nature of the planes: both Serra's realm and Phyrexia had been crafted by planeswalkers and would eventually melt back into chaos. Dominia, on the other hand, was natural and stable, and the lords of Phyrexia intended to conquer it before their own plane decayed.

Urza's travels next took him back to the Dominian world of Dominaria. He chose a remote island, Tolaria, as his base of operations and set up an academy there. In this school he gathered a body of scholars to study both magical and nonmagical phenomena. (One of the students, apparently a troublemaker, was a familiar name to veteran **Magic** players: Teferi, one of the central characters in the *Mirage*™ cycle.) Urza's goal was to build a time machine that he could use to travel back in time and prevent the creation of Phyrexia. However, this plan was doomed. The machine overloaded and exploded, sending bubbles of "fast" and "slow" time across the island and wrecking the academy. Urza abandoned his time-traveling schemes and journeyed next to the land of Shiv. In this plane, home of Shivan dragons and viashino lizardfolk, he learned a secret that he hopes will finally allow him to defeat the Phyrexians. This tantalizing hint is all we were given here—what the secret was remained to be told in the next expansion.

IMPORTANT CARDS

Along with a full slate of the staple "core cards" that are needed for any large expansion, the *Urza's Saga* set contained a number of powerful, environment-changing cards that inspired new deck types and made strong additions or alternative choices for existing types. Some of the most famous *Urza's Saga* cards include…

Tolarian Academy. The Academy seems innocent on the surface, but combine it with a fistful of zero-cost artifacts and a spell that untaps land, and you have a blue powerhouse. Decks built around this concept dominated 1998's Pro Tour–Rome.

Time Spiral. This card is a revision of Timetwister, one of the spells from the original **Magic** set banned from tournaments for being overpowered—but some players consider Time Spiral even stronger than the original! It costs six mana, which is difficult to obtain in most games, but if it resolves successfully it allows you to untap up to six lands, making it "free."

Worship. This white enchantment gives all your creatures the "Ali from Cairo" power—as long as you have a creature in play, damage will never remove your last 1 life.

Yawgmoth's Will. A major power card for black or part-black decks, Yawgmoth's Will allows you to play cards in your graveyard as if they were in your hand for one turn. If your opponent has a couple of Dark Rituals and a Drain Life in his or her graveyard, it's time to worry.

Lifeline. This card was misprinted in the English edition, so it required errata before the set was even

released. (The mistake was caught before the non-English editions went to press.) It's been referred to as the "*Urza's Saga* Ice Cauldron" due to the amount of rules confusion it created. Under *Fifth Edition*™ rules, it was an easy source for infinite loops.

Cradle Guard. Green received a number of powerful echo creatures; Cradle Guard became a quick favorite. A third-turn (or second-turn, with an Elf) 4/4 creature with trample creates quite a problem for most opponents!

Great Whale. The Whale was the straw that broke the camel's back in making Recurring Nightmare decks truly broken. Bring it into play, and it untaps the lands needed to replay Recurring Nightmare and a few extras, for an easy infinite-mana loop. (Peregrine Drake could do the same thing, but Great Whale was more impressive.)

Serra Avatar. The ultimate in big creatures, Serra Avatar raised a lot of eyebrows at the prerelease tournament. Because it can't stay in the graveyard to be reanimated however, it didn't prove as abusable as players initially feared.

ABSOLUTE GRACE
Versions: US:U
Current Errata: **none**

ABSOLUTE LAW
Versions: US:U
Current Errata: **none**

ABUNDANCE
Versions: US:R
Current Errata: **none**

ABYSSAL HORROR
Versions: US:R
Current Errata: **none**

ACADEMY RESEARCHERS
Versions: US:U
Current Errata: **none**

ACIDIC SOIL
Versions: US:U
Current Errata: **none**

ACRIDIAN
Versions: US:C
Current Errata: **none**

ALBINO TROLL
Versions: US:U
Current Errata: **none**

ANACONDA
Versions: PO:C, US:U
Current Errata: **none**

ANGELIC CHORUS
Versions: US:R
Current Errata: **none**

ANGELIC PAGE
Versions: US:C
Current Errata: **none**

ANNUL
Versions: US:C
Current Errata: **none**

ANTAGONISM
Versions: US:R
Current Errata: **none**

ARC LIGHTNING
Versions: US:C
Current Errata: **none**

ARCANE LABORATORY
Versions: US:U
Current Errata: **none**

ARGOTHIAN ELDER
Versions: US:U
Current Errata: **none**

ARGOTHIAN ENCHANTRESS
Versions: US:R
Current Errata: **none**

ARGOTHIAN SWINE
Versions: US:C
Current Errata: **none**

ARGOTHIAN WURM
Versions: US:R
Current Errata: **none**

ATTUNEMENT
Versions: US:R
Current Errata: **none**

BACK TO BASICS
Versions: US:R
Current Errata: **none**

BARRIN, MASTER WIZARD
Versions: US:R
Current Errata: **none**

BARRIN'S CODEX
Versions: US:R
Current Errata: **none**

BEDLAM
Versions: US:R
Current Errata: **none**

BEFOUL
Versions: US:C
Current Errata: **none**

BEREAVEMENT
Versions: US:U
Current Errata: **none**

BLANCHWOOD ARMOR
Versions: US:U
Current Errata: **none**

BLANCHWOOD TREEFOLK
Versions: US:C
Current Errata: **none**

BLASTED LANDSCAPE
Versions: US:U
Current Errata: **none**

BLOOD VASSAL
Versions: US:C
Current Errata: **none**

BOG RAIDERS
Versions: PO, US:C
Current Errata: **none**

BRAND
Versions: US:R
Current Errata: **none**

BRAVADO
Versions: US:C
Current Errata: **none**

BREACH
Versions: US:C
Current Errata: **none**

BRILLIANT HALO
Versions: US:C
Current Errata: **none**

BULL HIPPO
Versions: PO:C, US:U
Current Errata: **none**

Bulwark 3 {R}{R}

Enchantment

During your upkeep, Bulwark deals 1 damage to target opponent for each card in your hand greater than the number of cards in that player's hand.

"It will be the goblin's first bath, and its last." —Fire Eye, viashino bey

Illus. Brian Snoddy

BULWARK
Versions: **US:R**
Current Errata: **none**

Cackling Fiend 2{B}{B}

Summon Zombie

When Cackling Fiend comes into play, each of your opponents chooses and discards a card.

Its windpipe is only the first to amplify its maddening laughter.

Illus. Brian Despain   2/1

CACKLING FIEND
Versions: **US:C**
Current Errata: **none**

Carpet of Flowers {G}

Enchantment

During your main phase, you may add up to X mana of one color to your mana pool, where X is the number of islands target opponent controls.

Illus. Rebecca Guay

CARPET OF FLOWERS
Versions: **US:U**
Current Errata: **none**

Carrion Beetles {B}

Summon Insects

2 {B}, {T}: Remove from the game up to three target cards in one graveyard.

It's all fun and games until someone loses an eye.

Illus. Ron Spencer   1/1

CARRION BEETLES
Versions: **US:C**
Current Errata: **none**

Catalog 2{U}

Instant

Draw two cards, then choose and discard a card.

"Without order comes errors, and errors kill on Tolaria." —Barrin, master wizard

Illus. Berry

CATALOG
Versions: **US:C**
Current Errata: **none**

Catastrophe 4{W}{W}

Sorcery

Destroy all lands or all creatures. Creatures destroyed this way cannot regenerate this turn.

Radiant's eyes flashed. "Go, then," the angel spat at Serra, "and leave this world to those who truly care."

Illus. Andrey Robinson

CATASTROPHE
Versions: **US:R**
Current Errata: **none**

Cathodion 3

Artifact Creature

When Cathodion is put into a graveyard from play, add three colorless mana to your mana pool.

Instead of creating a tool that would be damaged by heat, the Thran built one that was charged by it.

Illus. Henry G. Higgenbotham   3/3

CATHODION
Versions: **US:U**
Current Errata: **none**

Cave Tiger 2{G}

Summon Cat

Whenever a creature blocks it, Cave Tiger gets +1/+1 until end of turn.

The druids found a haven in the cool limestone tunnels beneath Argoth. The invaders found only tigers.

Illus. Hannibal King   2/2

CAVE TIGER
Versions: **US:C**
Current Errata: **none**

Child of Gaea 3{G}{G}{G}

Summon Elemental

Trample

During your upkeep, pay {G}{G} or sacrifice Child of Gaea.

1 {G}: Regenerate Child of Gaea.

Illus. Paolo Parente   7/7

CHILD OF GAEA
Versions: **US:R**
Current Errata: **none**

Chimeric Staff 4

Artifact

{X}: Chimeric Staff is an artifact creature with power and toughness each equal to X until end of turn.

A snake in the grasp.

Illus. Michael Sutfin

CHIMERIC STAFF
Versions: **US:R**
Current Errata: **none**

Citanul Centaurs 3{G}

Summon Centaurs

Echo *(During your next upkeep after this permanent comes under your control, pay its casting cost or sacrifice it.)*

Citanul Centaurs cannot be the target of spells or abilities.

Illus. Val Mayerik   6/3

CITANUL CENTAURS
Versions: **US:R**
Current Errata: **none**

Citanul Flute 5

Artifact

{X}, {T}: Search your library for a creature card with total casting cost no greater than X. Reveal that card and put it into your hand. Shuffle your library afterward.

Illus. Berry

CITANUL FLUTE
Versions: **US:R**
Current Errata: **none**

CITANUL HIEROPHANTS
Versions: US:R
Current Errata: **none**

CLAWS OF GIX
Versions: US:U
Current Errata: **none**

CLEAR
Versions: US:U
Current Errata: **none**

CLOAK OF MISTS
Versions: US:C
Current Errata: **none**

CONFISCATE
Versions: US:U
Current Errata: **none**

CONGREGATE
Versions: US:C
Current Errata: **none**

CONTAMINATION
Versions: US:R
Current Errata: **none**

COPPER GNOMES
Versions: US:R
Current Errata: **none**

CORAL MERFOLK
Versions: US:C
Current Errata: **none**

CORRUPT
Versions: US:C
Current Errata: **none**

CRADLE GUARD
Versions: US:U
Current Errata: **none**

CRATER HELLION
Versions: US:R
Current Errata: **none**

CRAZED SKIRGE
Versions: **US:U**
Current Errata: **none**

CROSSWINDS
Versions: **US:U**
Current Errata: **none**

CRYSTAL CHIMES
Versions: **US:U**
Current Errata: **none**

CURFEW
Versions: **US:C**
Current Errata: **none**

DARK HATCHLING
Versions: **US:R**
Current Errata: **none**

DARK RITUAL
Versions: **A, B, UL, RV, 4E, 5E, IA, MI, TE, US:C**
Current Errata: **none**

DARKEST HOUR
Versions: **US:R**
Current Errata: **none**

DEFENSIVE FORMATION
Versions: **US:U**
Current Errata: **none**

DESPONDENCY
Versions: **US:C**
Current Errata: **none**

DESTRUCTIVE URGE
Versions: **US:U**
Current Errata: **none**

DIABOLIC SERVITUDE
Versions: **US:U**
Current Errata: **none**

DISCIPLE OF GRACE
Versions: **US:C**
Current Errata: **none**

DISCIPLE OF LAW
Versions: US:C
Current Errata: **none**

DISCORDANT DIRGE
Versions: US:R
Current Errata: **none**

DISENCHANT
Versions: A, B, UL, RV, 4E, 5E, IA, TE, US, 6E:C
Current Errata: **none**

DISORDER
Versions: US:U
Current Errata: **none**

DISRUPTIVE STUDENT
Versions: US:C
Current Errata: **none**

DOUSE
Versions: US:U
Current Errata: **none**

DRAGON BLOOD
Versions: US:U
Current Errata: **none**

DRIFTING DJINN
Versions: US:R
Current Errata: **none**

DRIFTING MEADOW
Versions: US:C
Current Errata: **none**

DROMOSAUR
Versions: US:C
Current Errata: **none**

DURESS
Versions: US:C
Current Errata: **none**

EASTERN PALADIN
Versions: US:R
Current Errata: **none**

ELECTRYTE
Versions: **US:R**
Current Errata: **none**

ELITE ARCHERS
Versions: **US:R**
Current Errata: **none**

ELVISH HERDER
Versions: **US:C**
Current Errata: **none**

ELVISH LYRIST
Versions: **US:C**
Current Errata: **none**

ENCHANTMENT ALTERATION
Versions: **US:U**
Current Errata: **none**

ENDLESS WURM
Versions: **US:R**
Current Errata: **none**

ENDOSKELETON
Versions: **US:U**
Current Errata: **none**

ENERGY FIELD
Versions: **US:R**
Current Errata: **none**

EXHAUSTION
Versions: **PO, SA, 3K:R, US:U**
Current Errata: **none**

EXHUME
Versions: **US:C**
Current Errata: **none**

EXPLORATION
Versions: **US:R**
Current Errata: **none**

EXPUNGE
Versions: **US:C**
Current Errata: **none**

FAITH HEALER
Versions: US:R
Current Errata: **none**

FALTER
Versions: US:C
Current Errata: **none**

FAULT LINE
Versions: US:R
Current Errata: **none**

FECUNDITY
Versions: US:U
Current Errata: **none**

FERTILE GROUND
Versions: US:C
Current Errata: **none**

FIERY MANTLE
Versions: US:C
Current Errata: **none**

FIRE ANTS
Versions: US:U
Current Errata: **none**

FLESH REAVER
Versions: US:U
Current Errata: **none**

FLUCTUATOR
Versions: US:R
Current Errata: **none**

FOG BANK
Versions: US:U
Current Errata: **none**

FOREST (VERSION 1)
Versions: US:L
Current Errata: **none**

FOREST (VERSION 2)
Versions: US:L
Current Errata: **none**

FOREST (VERSION 3)
Versions: **US:L**
Current Errata: **none**

FOREST (VERSION 4)
Versions: **US:L**
Current Errata: **none**

FORTITUDE
Versions: **US:C**
Current Errata: **none**

GAEA'S BOUNTY
Versions: **US:C**
Current Errata: **none**

GAEA'S CRADLE
Versions: **US:R**
Current Errata: **none**

GAEA'S EMBRACE
Versions: **US:U**
Current Errata: **none**

GAMBLE
Versions: **US:R**
Current Errata: **none**

GILDED DRAKE
Versions: **US:R**
Current Errata: **none**

GLORIOUS ANTHEM
Versions: **US:R**
Current Errata: **none**

GOBLIN CADETS
Versions: **US:U**
Current Errata: **none**

GOBLIN LACKEY
Versions: **US:U**
Current Errata: **none**

GOBLIN MATRON
Versions: **SA:U, US:C**
Current Errata: **none**

GOBLIN OFFENSIVE
Versions: US:U
Current Errata: **none**

GOBLIN PIKERS
Versions: US:C
Current Errata: **none**

GOBLIN RAIDER
Versions: SA, US:C
Current Errata: **none**

GOBLIN SPELUNKERS
Versions: US:C
Current Errata: **none**

GOBLIN WAR BUGGY
Versions: US:C
Current Errata: **none**

GORILLA WARRIOR
Versions: US:C
Current Errata: **none**

GRAFTED SKULLCAP
Versions: US:R
Current Errata: **none**

GREAT WHALE
Versions: US:R
Current Errata: **none**

GREATER GOOD
Versions: US:R
Current Errata: **none**

GREENER PASTURES
Versions: US:R
Current Errata: **none**

GUMA
Versions: US:U
Current Errata: **none**

HAWKEATER MOTH
Versions: US:U
Current Errata: **none**

HEADLONG RUSH
Versions: **US:C**
Current Errata: **none**

HEALING SALVE
Versions: **A, B, UL, RV, 4E, 5E, 6E, MI, US:C**
Current Errata: **none**

HEAT RAY
Versions: **US:C**
Current Errata: **none**

HERALD OF SERRA
Versions: **US:R**
Current Errata: **none**

HERMETIC STUDY
Versions: **US:C**
Current Errata: **none**

HIBERNATION
Versions: **US:U**
Current Errata: **none**

HIDDEN ANCIENTS
Versions: **US:U**
Current Errata: **none**

HIDDEN GUERRILLAS
Versions: **US:U**
Current Errata: **none**

HIDDEN HERD
Versions: **US:R**
Current Errata: **none**

HIDDEN PREDATORS
Versions: **US:R**
Current Errata: **none**

HIDDEN SPIDER
Versions: **US:C**
Current Errata: **none**

HIDDEN STAG
Versions: **US:R**
Current Errata: **none**

HOLLOW DOGS
Versions: **US:C**
Current Errata: **none**

HOPPING AUTOMATON
Versions: **US:U**
Current Errata: **none**

HORSESHOE CRAB
Versions: **US:C**
Current Errata: **none**

HUMBLE
Versions: **US:U**
Current Errata: **none**

HUSH
Versions: **US:C**
Current Errata: **none**

ILL-GOTTEN GAINS
Versions: **US:R**
Current Errata: **none**

IMAGINARY PET
Versions: **US:R**
Current Errata: **none**

INTREPID HERO
Versions: **US:R**
Current Errata: **none**

ISLAND (VERSION 1)
Versions: **US:L**
Current Errata: **none**

ISLAND (VERSION 2)
Versions: **US:L**
Current Errata: **none**

ISLAND (VERSION 3)
Versions: **US:L**
Current Errata: **none**

ISLAND (VERSION 4)
Versions: **US:L**
Current Errata: **none**

JAGGED LIGHTNING
Versions: SA, US:U
Current Errata: **none**

KARN, SILVER GOLEM
Versions: US:R
Current Errata: **none**

LAUNCH
Versions: US:C
Current Errata: **none**

LAY WASTE
Versions: US:C
Current Errata: **none**

LIFELINE
Versions: US:R
Current Errata: **none**

LIGHTNING DRAGON
Versions: US:R
Current Errata: **none**

LILTING REFRAIN
Versions: US:U
Current Errata: **none**

LINGERING MIRAGE
Versions: US:U
Current Errata: **none**

LOOMING SHADE
Versions: US:C
Current Errata: **none**

LOTUS BLOSSOM
Versions: US:R
Current Errata: **none**

LULL
Versions: US:C
Current Errata: **none**

LURKING EVIL
Versions: US:R
Current Errata: **none**

MANA LEECH
Versions: **US:U**
Current Errata: **none**

MELTDOWN
Versions: **US:U**
Current Errata: **none**

METROGNOME
Versions: **US:R**
Current Errata: **none**

MIDSUMMER REVEL
Versions: **US:R**
Current Errata: **none**

MISHRA'S HELIX
Versions: **US:R**
Current Errata: **none**

MOBILE FORT
Versions: **US:U**
Current Errata: **none**

MONK IDEALIST
Versions: **US:U**
Current Errata: **none**

MONK REALIST
Versions: **US:C**
Current Errata: **none**

MORPHLING
Versions: **US:R**
Current Errata: **none**

MOUNTAIN (VERSION 1)
Versions: **US:L**
Current Errata: **none**

MOUNTAIN (VERSION 2)
Versions: **US:L**
Current Errata: **none**

MOUNTAIN (VERSION 3)
Versions: **US:L**
Current Errata: **none**

MOUNTAIN (VERSION 4)
Versions: **US:L**
Current Errata: **none**

NO REST FOR THE WICKED
Versions: **US:U**
Current Errata: **none**

NOETIC SCALES
Versions: **US:R**
Current Errata: **none**

OKK
Versions: **US:R**
Current Errata: **none**

OPAL ACROLITH
Versions: **US:U**
Current Errata: **none**

OPAL ARCHANGEL
Versions: **US:R**
Current Errata: **none**

OPAL CARYATID
Versions: **US:C**
Current Errata: **none**

OPAL GARGOYLE
Versions: **US:C**
Current Errata: **none**

OPAL TITAN
Versions: **US:R**
Current Errata: **none**

OPPRESSION
Versions: **US:R**
Current Errata: **none**

ORDER OF YAWGMOTH
Versions: **US:U**
Current Errata: **none**

OUTMANEUVER
Versions: **US:U**
Current Errata: **none**

PACIFISM
Versions: MI, TE, 6E, US:C
Current Errata: **none**

PARASITIC BOND
Versions: US:U
Current Errata: **none**

PARIAH
Versions: US:R
Current Errata: **none**

PATH OF PEACE
Versions: US:C
Current Errata: **none**

PEGASUS CHARGER
Versions: US:C
Current Errata: **none**

PENDRELL DRAKE
Versions: US:C
Current Errata: **none**

PENDRELL FLUX
Versions: US:C
Current Errata: **none**

PEREGRINE DRAKE
Versions: US:U
Current Errata: **none**

PERSECUTE
Versions: US:R
Current Errata: **none**

PESTILENCE
Versions: A, B, UL, RV, 4E, 5E, 6E, IA, US:C
Current Errata: **none**

PHYREXIAN COLOSSUS
Versions: US:R
Current Errata: **none**

PHYREXIAN GHOUL
Versions: US:C
Current Errata: **none**

PHYREXIAN PROCESSOR
Versions: **US:R**
Current Errata: **none**

PHYREXIAN TOWER
Versions: **US:R**
Current Errata: **none**

PIT TRAP
Versions: **IA, US:U**
Current Errata: **none**

PLAINS (VERSION 1)
Versions: **US:L**
Current Errata: **none**

PLAINS (VERSION 2)
Versions: **US:L**
Current Errata: **none**

PLAINS (VERSION 3)
Versions: **US:L**
Current Errata: **none**

PLAINS (VERSION 4)
Versions: **US:L**
Current Errata: **none**

PLANAR BIRTH
Versions: **US:R**
Current Errata: **none**

PLANAR VOID
Versions: **US:U**
Current Errata: **none**

POLLUTED MIRE
Versions: **US:C**
Current Errata: **none**

POUNCING JAGUAR
Versions: **US:C**
Current Errata: **none**

POWER SINK
Versions: **MI, 5E, 6E, US:C**
Current Errata: **none**

POWER TAINT
Versions: **US:C**
Current Errata: **none**

PRESENCE OF THE MASTER
Versions: **US:U**
Current Errata: **none**

PRIEST OF GIX
Versions: **US:U**
Current Errata: **none**

PRIEST OF TITANIA
Versions: **US:C**
Current Errata: **none**

PURGING SCYTHE
Versions: **US:R**
Current Errata: **none**

RAIN OF FILTH
Versions: **US:U**
Current Errata: **none**

RAIN OF SALT
Versions: **US:U**
Current Errata: **none**

RAVENOUS SKIRGE
Versions: **US:C**
Current Errata: **none**

RAZE
Versions: **US:C**
Current Errata: **none**

RECANTATION
Versions: **US:R**
Current Errata: **none**

RECLUSIVE WIGHT
Versions: **US:U**
Current Errata: **none**

REDEEM
Versions: **US:U**
Current Errata: **none**

REFLEXES
Versions: **US:C**
Current Errata: **none**

REJUVENATE
Versions: **US:C**
Current Errata: **none**

REMEMBRANCE
Versions: **US:R**
Current Errata: **none**

REMOTE ISLE
Versions: **US:C**
Current Errata: **none**

REPROCESS
Versions: **US:R**
Current Errata: **none**

RESCIND
Versions: **US:C**
Current Errata: **none**

RETALIATION
Versions: **US:U**
Current Errata: **none**

RETROMANCER
Versions: **US:C**
Current Errata: **none**

REWIND
Versions: **US:C**
Current Errata: **none**

RUMBLING CRESCENDO
Versions: **US:R**
Current Errata: **none**

RUNE OF PROTECTION: ARTIFACTS
Versions: **US:U**
Current Errata: **none**

RUNE OF PROTECTION: BLACK
Versions: **US:C**
Current Errata: **none**

RUNE OF PROTECTION: BLUE
Versions: **US:C**
Current Errata: **none**

RUNE OF PROTECTION: GREEN
Versions: **US:C**
Current Errata: **none**

RUNE OF PROTECTION: LANDS
Versions: **US:R**
Current Errata: **none**

RUNE OF PROTECTION: RED
Versions: **US:C**
Current Errata: **none**

RUNE OF PROTECTION: WHITE
Versions: **US:C**
Current Errata: **none**

SANCTUM CUSTODIAN
Versions: **US:C**
Current Errata: **none**

SANCTUM GUARDIAN
Versions: **US:U**
Current Errata: **none**

SANDBAR MERFOLK
Versions: **US:C**
Current Errata: **none**

SANDBAR SERPENT
Versions: **US:U**
Current Errata: **none**

SANGUINE GUARD
Versions: **US:U**
Current Errata: **none**

SCALD
Versions: **US:U**
Current Errata: **none**

SCORIA WURM
Versions: **US:R**
Current Errata: **none**

SCRAP
Versions: **US:C**
Current Errata: **none**

SEASONED MARSHAL
Versions: **PO, US:U**
Current Errata: **none**

SERRA AVATAR
Versions: **US:R**
Current Errata: **none**

SERRA ZEALOT
Versions: **US:C**
Current Errata: **none**

SERRA'S EMBRACE
Versions: **US:U**
Current Errata: **none**

SERRA'S HYMN
Versions: **US:U**
Current Errata: **none**

SERRA'S LITURGY
Versions: **US:R**
Current Errata: **none**

SERRA'S SANCTUM
Versions: **US:R**
Current Errata: **none**

SHIMMERING BARRIER
Versions: **US:U**
Current Errata: **none**

SHIV'S EMBRACE
Versions: **US:U**
Current Errata: **none**

SHIVAN GORGE
Versions: **US:R**
Current Errata: **none**

SHIVAN HELLKITE
Versions: **US:R**
Current Errata: **none**

SHIVAN RAPTOR
Versions: US:U
Current Errata: none

SHOW AND TELL
Versions: US:R
Current Errata: none

SHOWER OF SPARKS
Versions: US:C
Current Errata: none

SICKEN
Versions: US:C
Current Errata: none

SILENT ATTENDANT
Versions: US:C
Current Errata: none

SKIRGE FAMILIAR
Versions: US:U
Current Errata: none

SKITTERING SKIRGE
Versions: US:C
Current Errata: none

SLEEPER AGENT
Versions: US:R
Current Errata: none

SLIPPERY KARST
Versions: US:C
Current Errata: none

SMOKESTACK
Versions: US:R
Current Errata: none

SMOLDERING CRATER
Versions: US:C
Current Errata: none

SNEAK ATTACK
Versions: US:R
Current Errata: none

SOMNOPHORE
Versions: **US:R**
Current Errata: **none**

SONGSTITCHER
Versions: **US:U**
Current Errata: **none**

SOUL SCULPTOR
Versions: **US:R**
Current Errata: **none**

SPINED FLUKE
Versions: **US:U**
Current Errata: **none**

SPIRE OWL
Versions: **US:U**
Current Errata: **none**

SPOROGENESIS
Versions: **US:R**
Current Errata: **none**

SPREADING ALGAE
Versions: **US:U**
Current Errata: **none**

STEAM BLAST
Versions: **US:U**
Current Errata: **none**

STERN PROCTOR
Versions: **US:U**
Current Errata: **none**

STROKE OF GENIUS
Versions: **US:R**
Current Errata: **none**

SULFURIC VAPORS
Versions: **US:R**
Current Errata: **none**

SUNDER
Versions: **US:R**
Current Errata: **none**

SWAMP (VERSION 1)
Versions: US:L
Current Errata: **none**

SWAMP (VERSION 2)
Versions: US:L
Current Errata: **none**

SWAMP (VERSION 3)
Versions: US:L
Current Errata: **none**

SWAMP (VERSION 4)
Versions: US:L
Current Errata: **none**

SYMBIOSIS
Versions: US:C
Current Errata: **none**

TAINTED ÆTHER
Versions: US:R
Current Errata: **none**

TELEPATHY
Versions: US:U
Current Errata: **none**

TEMPORAL APERTURE
Versions: US:R
Current Errata: **none**

THRAN QUARRY
Versions: US:R
Current Errata: **none**

THRAN TURBINE
Versions: US:U
Current Errata: **none**

THUNDERING GIANT
Versions: US:U
Current Errata: **none**

TIME SPIRAL
Versions: US:R
Current Errata: **none**

TITANIA'S BOON
Versions: **US:U**
Current Errata: **none**

TITANIA'S CHOSEN
Versions: **US:U**
Current Errata: **none**

TOLARIAN ACADEMY
Versions: **US:R**
Current Errata: **none**

TOLARIAN WINDS
Versions: **US:C**
Current Errata: **none**

TORCH SONG
Versions: **US:U**
Current Errata: **none**

TREEFOLK SEEDLINGS
Versions: **US:U**
Current Errata: **none**

TREETOP RANGERS
Versions: **US:C**
Current Errata: **none**

TURNABOUT
Versions: **US:U**
Current Errata: **none**

UMBILICUS
Versions: **US:R**
Current Errata: **none**

UNNERVE
Versions: **US:C**
Current Errata: **none**

UNWORTHY DEAD
Versions: **US:C**
Current Errata: **none**

URZA'S ARMOR
Versions: **US:U**
Current Errata: **none**

VAMPIRIC EMBRACE
Versions: **US:U**
Current Errata: **none**

VEBULID
Versions: **US:R**
Current Errata: **none**

VEIL OF BIRDS
Versions: **US:C**
Current Errata: **none**

VEILED APPARITION
Versions: **US:U**
Current Errata: **none**

VEILED CROCODILE
Versions: **US:R**
Current Errata: **none**

VEILED SENTRY
Versions: **US:U**
Current Errata: **none**

VEILED SERPENT
Versions: **US:C**
Current Errata: **none**

VENOMOUS FANGS
Versions: **US:C**
Current Errata: **none**

VERNAL BLOOM
Versions: **US:R**
Current Errata: **none**

VIASHINO OUTRIDER
Versions: **US:C**
Current Errata: **none**

VIASHINO RUNNER
Versions: **US:C**
Current Errata: **none**

VIASHINO SANDSWIMMER
Versions: **US:R**
Current Errata: **none**

VIASHINO WEAPONSMITH
Versions: **US:C**
Current Errata: **none**

VICTIMIZE
Versions: **US:U**
Current Errata: **none**

VILE REQUIEM
Versions: **US:U**
Current Errata: **none**

VOICE OF GRACE
Versions: **US:U**
Current Errata: **none**

VOICE OF LAW
Versions: **US:U**
Current Errata: **none**

VOLTAIC KEY
Versions: **US:U**
Current Errata: **none**

VUG LIZARD
Versions: **US:U**
Current Errata: **none**

WALL OF JUNK
Versions: **US:U**
Current Errata: **none**

WAR DANCE
Versions: **US:U**
Current Errata: **none**

WAYLAY
Versions: **US:U**
Current Errata: **none**

WESTERN PALADIN
Versions: **US:R**
Current Errata: **none**

WHETSTONE
Versions: **US:R**
Current Errata: **none**

WHIRLWIND
Versions: US:R
Current Errata: **none**

WILD DOGS
Versions: US:C
Current Errata: **none**

WILDFIRE
Versions: US:R
Current Errata: **none**

WINDFALL
Versions: US:U
Current Errata: **none**

WINDING WURM
Versions: US:C
Current Errata: **none**

WIRECAT
Versions: US:U
Current Errata: **none**

WITCH ENGINE
Versions: US:R
Current Errata: **none**

WIZARD MENTOR
Versions: US:C
Current Errata: **none**

WORN POWERSTONE
Versions: US:U
Current Errata: **none**

WORSHIP
Versions: US:R
Current Errata: **none**

YAWGMOTH'S EDICT
Versions: US:U
Current Errata: **none**

YAWGMOTH'S WILL
Versions: US:R
Current Errata: **none**

ZEPHID
Versions: **US:R**
Current Errata: **none**

ZEPHID'S EMBRACE
Versions: **US:U**
Current Errata: **none**

OVERVIEW

The *Urza's Legacy*™ expansion, the second set in the Urza cycle, followed up and enlarged on many of the themes first introduced in the *Urza's Saga* set and added a few minor themes. It contained a number of good, solid cards for both Sealed-Deck and Constructed play along with a few that really stood out.

The two *Urza's Saga* mechanics, echo and cycling, are both present in *Urza's Legacy* cards as well. In the earlier set, echo was solely a creature ability; The *Urza's Legacy* set expanded this by including two artifacts (Ring of Gix and Thran Weaponry) with echo.

This expansion also continued the themes of "sleeping" and "eternal" enchantments, adding a handful of new cards of each type. It also included a set of enchantments that

function like the sleepers but sacrifice themselves to produce some effect when the condition is met rather than turning into a creature. They're essentially "sleeping instants." This was not an entirely new concept, since a few isolated cards like this had appeared in the past, but here it's a significant subtheme.

The other significant *Urza's Legacy* card cycle was its lands. For each color, there was a land that could tap for that color of mana or temporarily turn itself into a creature. These can be used for many of the same purposes as the out-of-print Mishra's Factory.

KEY CARDS

Memory Jar. This was the first card to be banned from tournament play by the DCI™ players' organization before it had been proven to be broken in tournament use. Many players contacted the DCI after the set was released, showing how Memory Jar made first-turn wins possible and second- to third-turn wins common in the Standard environment.

Multani's Presence. Green mages couldn't praise this color-hoser enough. Play it on turn one, before your blue opponents have counter-spell capability, and watch them gnash their teeth in frustration as every counterspell they play gives you greater card advantage.

Ring of Gix. This is the new replacement for Icy Manipulator. Ring of Gix costs two more mana than Icy

in total, but this cost is spread over two turns; you can play and use it a turn earlier than you could an Icy.

Palinchron. This "free" creature immediately replaced Great Whale as

the favorite for Recurring Nightmare–Survival of the Fittest infinite-mana recursion decks. The party was short-lived, though, since the DCI eventually issued errata changing all the "free" creatures so that they untapped lands only if the creature was actually played.

Faerie Conclave, **Forbidding Watchtower**, **Ghitu Encampment**, **Spawning Pool**, and **Treetop Village**. As mentioned before, these lands that turn into creatures can fill many of the same needs that Mishra's Factory did, making them welcome additions to several deck types.

Second Chance. Here's a variation of Time Walk that gives your opponent advance warning and (usually) a full turn to do something about it. At first, Second Chance made a game-winning combination with anything that could bounce it back to your hand (such as Capsize). However, all the "sleeping instant" enchantments were soon given errata so they only produce their effect if the enchantment is actually sacrificed.

Purify. This sorcery completed white's suite of "reset buttons." Now white can do global destruction of all four permanent types.

Multani, Maro-Sorcerer. This super-Maro is costly but definitely worth the price. And that's in single-player games. In multiplayer it becomes obscenely powerful. Of course, this may backfire, as the other players may all gang up on the player who has Multani.

Defense Grid. This is a favorite sideboard card for fast decks against blue opponents. By the time the blue player has enough mana to get a counterspell past the Defense Grid, the game is over (or close to it).

THE STORY

The *Urza's Legacy* story picks up right where the *Urza's Saga* story left off, as Urza works on his master plan to defeat the Phyrexians. The secret hinted at in the earlier set is revealed: the Shivan mana rig can be used to create powerstones, energy units that can power artifacts and even aid in planar travel. Urza manages to make peace between the native goblins and

viashino and sets them to building powerstones and the framework of what will eventually become the flying ship *Weatherlight*.

Meanwhile, Tolaria continues to be very chaotic. Many of the residents are trapped in bubbles of slow or fast time. In one of the fast bubbles, a Phyrexian sleeper agent named Kerrick works at evolving himself and his squad of negators, recycling and rebuilding as only machine-based creatures can do, with plans of eventually breaking out and wreaking havoc.

While the goblins and viashino work on construction, Urza travels to Yavimaya to enlist the aid of the sentient forest. This proves more difficult than he'd expected, though, because the forest still had dark memories of the destruction of Argoth in the Brothers' War. The Maro-sorcerer Multani captures Urza and merges his consciousness with that of the Yavimaya forest, forcing him to experience Argoth's destruction personally but also allowing the forest to experience Urza's memories of Phyrexia. This

communion lasts for several years, until Kerrick breaks free of the time bubble in Tolaria. Urza gathers all the Shivan and Tolarian forces he can and, with the help of Multani, eventually manages to destroy Kerrick and his minions. This convinces Yavimaya to aid him by giving him the Weatherseed, an organic construct that will grow around the Thran metal framework to form a hull for the *Weatherlight*.

Urza's next problem is charging the powerstone. His research has uncovered only one way this can be done: he must convert an entire artificially created plane to energy and capture it inside the stone. He knows of one such plane that is close to collapse: the realm created by the planeswalker Serra. He returns there and finds that the Phyrexian assault has accelerated its decay, leaving it even more unstable than he'd guessed. He attempts to evacuate the remaining inhabitants but is opposed by the archangel Radiant. This leads to another massive battle. As the realm crumbles, Urza rescues as many of the refugees as he can, then folds the plane's energies into the *Weatherlight*'s powerstone with Radiant and some of her forces still trapped inside.

With the artifact parts of the Legacy now nearly complete, Urza's last task remains: to forge the Legacy's human component. The story will continue in the *Urza's Destiny*™ card set.

ABOUT FACE
Versions: UL:C
Current Errata: **none**

ANGEL'S TRUMPET
Versions: UL:U
Current Errata: **none**

ANGELIC CURATOR
Versions: UL:C
Current Errata: **none**

ANTHROPLASM
Versions: UL:R
Current Errata: **none**

ARCHIVIST
Versions: UL:C
Current Errata: **none**

AURA FLUX
Versions: UL:C
Current Errata: **none**

AVALANCHE RIDERS
Versions: UL:U
Current Errata: **none**

BEAST OF BURDEN
Versions: UL:R
Current Errata: **none**

BLESSED REVERSAL
Versions: UL:R
Current Errata: **none**

BLOATED TOAD
Versions: UL:U
Current Errata: **none**

BONE SHREDDER
Versions: UL:U
Current Errata: **none**

BOUNCING BEEBLES
Versions: UL:C
Current Errata: **none**

BRINK OF MADNESS
Versions: **UL:R**
Current Errata: **none**

BURST OF ENERGY
Versions: **UL:C**
Current Errata: **none**

CESSATION
Versions: **UL:C**
Current Errata: **none**

CLOUD OF FAERIES
Versions: **UL:C**
Current Errata: **none**

CRAWLSPACE
Versions: **UL:R**
Current Errata: **none**

CROP ROTATION
Versions: **UL:C**
Current Errata: **none**

DAMPING ENGINE
Versions: **UL:R**
Current Errata: **none**

DARKWATCH ELVES
Versions: **UL:U**
Current Errata: **none**

DEFENDER OF CHAOS
Versions: **UL:C**
Current Errata: **none**

DEFENDER OF LAW
Versions: **UL:C**
Current Errata: **none**

DEFENSE GRID
Versions: **UL:R**
Current Errata: **none**

DEFENSE OF THE HEART
Versions: **UL:R**
Current Errata: **none**

DELUSIONS OF MEDIOCRITY
Versions: UL:R
Current Errata: **none**

DERANGED HERMIT
Versions: UL:R
Current Errata: **none**

DEVOUT HARPIST
Versions: UL:C
Current Errata: **none**

ENGINEERED PLAGUE
Versions: UL:U
Current Errata: **none**

ERASE
Versions: UL:C
Current Errata: **none**

EVISCERATOR
Versions: UL:R
Current Errata: **none**

EXPENDABLE TROOPS
Versions: UL:C
Current Errata: **none**

FAERIE CONCLAVE
Versions: UL:LU
Current Errata: **none**

FLEETING IMAGE
Versions: UL:R
Current Errata: **none**

FOG OF GNATS
Versions: UL:C
Current Errata: **none**

FORBIDDING WATCHTOWER
Versions: UL:LU
Current Errata: **none**

FRANTIC SEARCH
Versions: UL:C
Current Errata: **none**

GANG OF ELK
Versions: UL:R
Current Errata: **none**

GHITU ENCAMPMENT
Versions: UL:C
Current Errata: **none**

GHITU FIRE-EATER
Versions: UL:U
Current Errata: **none**

GHITU SLINGER
Versions: UL:C
Current Errata: **none**

GHITU WAR CRY
Versions: UL:U
Current Errata: **none**

GIANT COCKROACH
Versions: UL:C
Current Errata: **none**

GOBLIN MEDICS
Versions: UL:C
Current Errata: **none**

GOBLIN WELDER
Versions: UL:R
Current Errata: **none**

GRANITE GRIP
Versions: UL:C
Current Errata: **none**

GRIM MONOLITH
Versions: UL:R
Current Errata: **none**

HARMONIC CONVERGENCE
Versions: UL:U
Current Errata: **none**

HIDDEN GIBBONS
Versions: UL:R
Current Errata: **none**

HOPE AND GLORY
Versions: UL:U
Current Errata: **none**

IMPENDING DISASTER
Versions: UL:R
Current Errata: **none**

INTERVENE
Versions: UL:C
Current Errata: **none**

IRON MAIDEN
Versions: UL:R
Current Errata: **none**

IRON WILL
Versions: UL:C
Current Errata: **none**

JHOIRA'S TOOLBOX
Versions: UL:U
Current Errata: **none**

KARMIC GUIDE
Versions: UL:R
Current Errata: **none**

KING CRAB
Versions: UL:U
Current Errata: **none**

KNIGHTHOOD
Versions: UL:U
Current Errata: **none**

LAST-DITCH EFFORT
Versions: UL:U
Current Errata: **none**

LAVA AXE
Versions: UL:C
Current Errata: **none**

LEVITATION
Versions: UL:U
Current Errata: **none**

LONE WOLF
Versions: **UL:U**
Current Errata: **none**

LURKING SKIRGE
Versions: **UL:R**
Current Errata: **none**

MARTYR'S CAUSE
Versions: **UL:U**
Current Errata: **none**

MEMORY JAR
Versions: **UL:R**
Current Errata: **none**

MIGHT OF OAKS
Versions: **UL:R**
Current Errata: **none**

MISCALCULATION
Versions: **UL:C**
Current Errata: **none**

MOLTEN HYDRA
Versions: **UL:R**
Current Errata: **none**

MOTHER OF RUNES
Versions: **UL:U**
Current Errata: **none**

MULTANI, MARO-SORCERER
Versions: **UL:R**
Current Errata: **none**

MULTANI'S ACOLYTE
Versions: **UL:C**
Current Errata: **none**

MULTANI'S PRESENCE
Versions: **UL:U**
Current Errata: **none**

NO MERCY
Versions: **UL:R**
Current Errata: **none**

OPAL AVENGER
Versions: UL:R
Current Errata: **none**

OPAL CHAMPION
Versions: UL:C
Current Errata: **none**

OPPORTUNITY
Versions: UL:U
Current Errata: **none**

OSTRACIZE
Versions: UL:C
Current Errata: **none**

PALINCHRON
Versions: UL:R
Current Errata: **none**

PARCH
Versions: UL:C
Current Errata: **none**

PEACE AND QUIET
Versions: UL:U
Current Errata: **none**

PHYREXIAN BROODLINGS
Versions: UL:C
Current Errata: **none**

PHYREXIAN DEBASER
Versions: UL:C
Current Errata: **none**

PHYREXIAN DEFILER
Versions: UL:U
Current Errata: **none**

PHYREXIAN DENOUNCER
Versions: UL:C
Current Errata: **none**

PHYREXIAN PLAGUELORD
Versions: UL:R
Current Errata: **none**

PHYREXIAN RECLAMATION
Versions: **UL:U**
Current Errata: **none**

PLAGUE BEETLE
Versions: **UL:C**
Current Errata: **none**

PLANAR COLLAPSE
Versions: **UL:R**
Current Errata: **none**

PURIFY
Versions: **UL:R**
Current Errata: **none**

PYGMY PYROSAUR
Versions: **UL:C**
Current Errata: **none**

PYROMANCY
Versions: **UL:R**
Current Errata: **none**

QUICKSILVER AMULET
Versions: **UL:R**
Current Errata: **none**

RACK AND RUIN
Versions: **UL:U**
Current Errata: **none**

RADIANT, ARCHANGEL
Versions: **UL:R**
Current Errata: **none**

RADIANT'S DRAGOONS
Versions: **UL:U**
Current Errata: **none**

RADIANT'S JUDGMENT
Versions: **UL:C**
Current Errata: **none**

RANCOR
Versions: **UL:C**
Current Errata: **none**

RANK AND FILE
Versions: **UL:U**
Current Errata: **none**

RAVEN FAMILIAR
Versions: **UL:U**
Current Errata: **none**

REBUILD
Versions: **UL:U**
Current Errata: **none**

REPOPULATE
Versions: **UL:C**
Current Errata: **none**

RING OF GIX
Versions: **UL:R**
Current Errata: **none**

RIVALRY
Versions: **UL:R**
Current Errata: **none**

SCRAPHEAP
Versions: **UL:R**
Current Errata: **none**

SECOND CHANCE
Versions: **UL:R**
Current Errata: **none**

SHIVAN PHOENIX
Versions: **UL:R**
Current Errata: **none**

SICK AND TIRED
Versions: **UL:C**
Current Errata: **none**

SILK NET
Versions: **UL:C**
Current Errata: **none**

SIMIAN GRUNTS
Versions: **UL:C**
Current Errata: **none**

SLEEPER'S GUILE
Versions: **UL:C**
Current Errata: **none**

SLOW MOTION
Versions: **UL:C**
Current Errata: **none**

SLUGGISHNESS
Versions: **UL:C**
Current Errata: **none**

SNAP
Versions: **UL:C**
Current Errata: **none**

SPAWNING POOL
Versions: **UL:LU**
Current Errata: **none**

SUBVERSION
Versions: **UL:R**
Current Errata: **none**

SUSTAINER OF THE REALM
Versions: **UL:U**
Current Errata: **none**

SWAT
Versions: **UL:C**
Current Errata: **none**

TETHERED SKIRGE
Versions: **UL:U**
Current Errata: **none**

THORNWIND FAERIES
Versions: **UL:C**
Current Errata: **none**

THRAN LENS
Versions: **UL:R**
Current Errata: **none**

THRAN WAR MACHINE
Versions: **UL:U**
Current Errata: **none**

THRAN WEAPONRY
Versions: **UL:R**
Current Errata: **none**

TICKING GNOMES
Versions: **UL:U**
Current Errata: **none**

TINKER
Versions: **UL:U**
Current Errata: **none**

TRAGIC POET
Versions: **UL:C**
Current Errata: **none**

TREACHEROUS LINK
Versions: **UL:U**
Current Errata: **none**

TREEFOLK MYSTIC
Versions: **UL:C**
Current Errata: **none**

TREETOP VILLAGE
Versions: **UL:U**
Current Errata: **none**

UNEARTH
Versions: **UL:C**
Current Errata: **none**

URZA'S BLUEPRINTS
Versions: **UL:R**
Current Errata: **none**

VIASHINO BEY
Versions: **UL:C**
Current Errata: **none**

VIASHINO CUTTHROAT
Versions: **UL:U**
Current Errata: **none**

VIASHINO HERETIC
Versions: **UL:U**
Current Errata: **none**

VIASHINO SANDSCOUT
Versions: UL:C
Current Errata: **none**

VIGILANT DRAKE
Versions: UL:C
Current Errata: **none**

WALKING SPONGE
Versions: UL:U
Current Errata: **none**

WEATHERSEED ELF
Versions: UL:C
Current Errata: **none**

WEATHERSEED FAERIES
Versions: UL:C
Current Errata: **none**

WEATHERSEED TREEFOLK
Versions: UL:R
Current Errata: **none**

WHEEL OF TORTURE
Versions: UL:R
Current Errata: **none**

WING SNARE
Versions: UL:U
Current Errata: **none**

YAVIMAYA GRANGER
Versions: UL:C
Current Errata: **none**

YAVIMAYA SCION
Versions: UL:C
Current Errata: **none**

YAVIMAYA WURM
Versions: UL:C
Current Errata: **none**

CLASSIC

™

OVERVIEW

The *Classic*™ (Sixth Edition) set marked a major revolution—or evolution—in **Magic: The Gathering®** rules. Through the years, the **Magic** rules had gone through many changes, but these were mostly just grafted onto the existing rules. Now, for the first time, the rules were rewritten from the ground up. The cards were rewritten to correspond with the new rules, and the rules team also released updated wordings for all previously printed cards.

The biggest changes in the *Classic* rules were in spell timing and damage prevention, two areas that had become quite convoluted. A major goal of the rewrite was to have all spells and abilities played by a single set of rules rather than half a dozen different ones. This meant that some spells and abilities previously played only in special windows could now be played at any time. Damage prevention and regeneration now had to be played before the event they wanted to modify took place. All spells and abilities, including triggered abilities, shared a single resolution stack. New spells could be played in response to resolutions, rather than the "batch" structure used in the *Fifth Edition* and earlier rules. They could also be played in response to triggered abilities, which used to be illegal. The card types "interrupt" and "mana source" and the corresponding timing windows were entirely eliminated; under the new rules, they both became instants.

In order for the new damage prevention to interact properly with combat damage, combat damage was also changed to go on the stack. This made creatures that could bounce themselves back to your hand or sacrifice themselves for some useful ability much more valuable than they had been previously, since using these abilities no longer prevented the cards from dealing their combat damage.

Another sweeping change was the elimination of phase costs and phase abilities. All of these were changed to regular triggered abilities that triggered at the beginning of a phase or step. If such an ability entered play or came into effect later in the phase, it wouldn't do anything until the following turn. This eliminated almost

all the "infinite loop" combinations that used to cause rules headaches. The few remaining were handled by a new rule: any true infinite loop causes the game to end in a draw.

Other miscellaneous changes included the 0-life rule and the tapped-artifact rule. Instead of waiting until the end of a phase, a player who reaches 0 life loses immediately. And tapped artifacts no longer have most of their abilities shut off. A few artifacts such as Winter Orb received errata adding a "while untapped" clause, but most were left alone.

KEY CARDS

As has become customary for revisions of the main set, the *Classic* set rotated out a number of the cards from the *Fifth Edition* printing, replacing them with different cards from more recent expansions that had gone out of print. Here are some highlights.

Uktabi Orangutan. This card was one of the most popular green creatures ever. It's frequently splashed into other color decks to help with artifact control. It's also a favorite to combine with Recurring Nightmare.

Stupor. Black mages were happy to see this strong discard-forcing spell return to the play environment.

Sage Owl. This creature is often overlooked, but several of the top tournament players have commented on its value. It combines very well with blue's other library-manipulation and card-drawing effects.

Staunch Defenders. A fat white creature that also gives a life bonus. This card is most popular with combinations that can bounce it in and out of play multiple times, such as Tradewind Riders and Recurring Nightmare.

The Tutors: Enlightened, Mystical, Vampiric, and Worldly. These are priceless for combo deck

because they allow you to dig out the card you need to complete the combo. Vampiric Tutor is the favorite, as it's the most flexible, but the others are also of tournament quality.

Deflection. A twist on blue's usual ability, this one can turn a spell back on its controller or redirect a useful enchantment from your opponent's creature to your own.

Desertion. Another twist on the standard counterspell, Desertion combines countering with a control effect, giving you card advantage and often wrecking your opponent's strategy.

Hammer of Bogardan. Reusable direct damage is very potent, even at this high price. Hammer of Bogardan also gives counterspell-based decks fits, since it keeps coming back. The Hammer forces players to consider including some spells in their decks that remove cards from the game.

Snake Basket. This creature-generating artifact is popular both in "fun" decks and in certain tournament decks that generate lots of mana.

Final Fortune. The "do or die" version of Time Walk, this card makes a strong addition to many red decks. Some combination decks that "go off" to win in one big flurry of action also use it; the loss at end of turn is no penalty, since these decks lose anyway if the combination fails.

Relentless Assault. For creature-based decks, this is almost another Time Walk. With this and Final Fortune in the set, red mages can potentially catch an opponent completely unprepared by making several attacks in a row.

Creeping Mold. This is a flexible card that can destroy almost anything at a reasonable price. It goes a long way toward making green control decks feasible.

River Boa. This is one of the best small green creatures ever printed. River Boa is worth considering even against non-blue opponents, and against blue it's just plain excellent.

Derelor. A favorite for the "fat black" style of deck and also for multicolored play. Yes, it makes your black spells cost more, but as long as you have a 4/4 creature in play you usually don't need to play much else.

Some significant *Fifth Edition* cards that are NOT in this set:

Nevinyrral's Disk. This was often used in black or blue decks to give them a way to destroy enchantments. With its removal, the strengths and weaknesses of the colors become more important.

Winter Orb and Stasis. Removing these prevents "prison" style decks that lock the game down into a no-mana crawl. Sixth Edition tries to promote a more interactive game.

Bad Moon. The decision to remove Bad Moon but leave Crusade left a lot of players scratching their heads. Perhaps the designers wanted to make black and white weenie decks

more distinct instead of having so many mirrored spells.

Hydroblast and Pyroblast. These color-specific counterspells were near-automatic sideboard choices for red and blue decks. Counterspells are out of flavor for red, however, and blue has a number of other choices.

Ball Lightning and Incinerate. Over the past year or so, "Sligh" decks (fast mono-red creature burn) had become a bit too fast. The designers hoped that removing a few of the most often-used damage sources from the environment would put on the brakes just enough while still leaving it a valid deck type.

Necropotence. This enchantment's inclusion in the *Fifth Edition* set caused a great deal of controversy. Removing it from the *Classic* rotation caused just as much. However, Necrologia in the *Tempest*™ cycle provides an adequate replacement in most cases.

ABDUCTION
Versions: **WE, 6E: U**
Current Errata: **none**

ABYSSAL HUNTER
Versions: **MI, 6E: R**
Current Errata: **none**

ABYSSAL SPECTER
Versions: **IA, 5E, 6E U**
Current Errata: **none**

ADARKAR WASTES
Versions: **IA, 5E, 6E: R**
Current Errata: **none**

ÆTHER FLASH
Versions: **WE, 6E: U**
Current Errata: **none**

AGONIZING MEMORIES
Versions: **WE, 6E: U**
Current Errata: **none**

AIR ELEMENTAL
Versions: **A, B, UL, RV, 4E, 5E, 6E: U**
Current Errata: **none**

ALADDIN'S RING
Versions: **AN: U, A, B, UL, RV, 4E, 5E, 6E: R**
Current Errata: **none**

AMBER PRISON
Versions: **MI, 6E: R**
Current Errata: **none**

ANABA BODYGUARD
Versions: **HL, 6E: C**
Current Errata: **none**

ANABA SHAMAN
Versions: **HL, 6E: C**
Current Errata: **none**

ANCESTRAL MEMORIES
Versions: **MI, 6E: R**
Current Errata: **none**

ANIMATE WALL
Versions: A, B, UL, RV, 4E, 5E, 6E: R
Current Errata: **none**

ANKH OF MISHRA
Versions: A, B, UL, RV, 4E, 5E, 6E: R
Current Errata: **none**

ARCHANGEL
Versions: VI, 6E: R
Current Errata: **none**

ARDENT MILITIA
Versions: WE, 6E: C
Current Errata: **none**

ARMAGEDDON
Versions: A, B, UL, RV, 4E, 5E, 6E: R
Current Errata: **none**

ARMORED PEGASUS
Versions: TE, 6E: C
Current Errata: **none**

ASHEN POWDER
Versions: MI, 6E: R
Current Errata: **none**

ASHNOD'S ALTAR
Versions: AN: U, CH: C, 5E, 6E: U
Current Errata: **none**

BALDUVIAN BARBARIANS
Versions: IA, 6E: C
Current Errata: **none**

BALDUVIAN HORDE
Versions: AL, 6E: R
Current Errata: **none**

BIRDS OF PARADISE
Versions: A, B, UL, RV, 4E, 5E, 6E: R
Current Errata: **none**

BLAZE
Versions: PO:C, SA, 3K: U, 6E:U
Current Errata: **none**

BLIGHT
Versions: LG, 4E, 5E, 6E: U
Current Errata: **none**

BLIGHTED SHAMAN
Versions: MI, 6E: U
Current Errata: **none**

BLOOD PET
Versions: TE, 6E: C
Current Errata: **none**

BOG IMP
Versions: DK, 4E, 5E, 6E: C
Current Errata: **none**

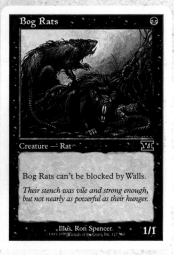

BOG RATS
Versions: DK, CH, 5E, 6E: C
Current Errata: **none**

BOG WRAITH
Versions: A, B, UL, RV, 4E, 5E, 6E: U
Current Errata: **none**

BOIL
Versions: TE, 6E: U
Current Errata: **none**

BOOMERANG
Versions: LG, CH, MI, 5E, 6E: C
Current Errata: **none**

BOTTLE OF SULEIMAN
Versions: AN, RV, 4E, 5E, 6E: R
Current Errata: **none**

BROWSE
Versions: AL, 6E: U
Current Errata: **none**

BRUSHLAND
Versions: IA, 5E, 6E: R
Current Errata: **none**

BURROWING
Versions: A, B, UL, RV, 4E, 6E: U
Current Errata: **none**

CALL OF THE WILD
Versions: WE, 6E: R
Current Errata: none

CASTLE
Versions: A, B, UL, RV, 4E, 5E, 6E:U
Current Errata: none

CAT WARRIORS
Versions: LG, CH, 5E, 6E: C
Current Errata: none

CELESTIAL DAWN
Versions: MI, 6E: R
Current Errata: none

CHARCOAL DIAMOND
Versions: MI, 6E: U
Current Errata: none

CHILL
Versions: TE, 6E: U
Current Errata: none

CIRCLE OF PROTECTION: BLACK
Versions: A, B, UL, RV, IA, 4E, 5E, TE, 6E: C
Current Errata: none

CIRCLE OF PROTECTION: BLUE
Versions: A, B, UL, RV, IA, 4E, 5E, TE, 6E: C
Current Errata: none

CIRCLE OF PROTECTION: GREEN
Versions: A, B, UL, RV, IA, 4E, 5E, TE, 6E: C
Current Errata: none

CIRCLE OF PROTECTION: RED
Versions: A, B, UL, RV, IA, 4E, 5E, TE, 6E: C
Current Errata: none

CIRCLE OF PROTECTION: WHITE
Versions: A, B, UL, RV, IA, 4E, 5E, TE, 6E: C
Current Errata: none

CITY OF BRASS
Versions: AN, CH, 5E, 6E: R
Current Errata: none

COERCION
Versions: VI, TE, 6E: C
Current Errata: **none**

CONQUER
Versions: IA, 5E, 6E: U
Current Errata: **none**

COUNTERSPELL
Versions: A, B, UL, RV, IA, 4E, 5E, TE, 6E: C
Current Errata: **none**

CREEPING MOLD
Versions: VI, 6E: U
Current Errata: **none**

CRIMSON HELLKITE
Versions: MI, 6E: R
Current Errata: **none**

CRUSADE
Versions: A, B, UL, RV, 4E, 5E, 6E:U
Current Errata: **none**

CRYSTAL ROD
Versions: A, B, UL, RV, 4E, 5E, 6E: U
Current Errata: **none**

CRYSTAL VEIN
Versions: MI, 6E: U
Current Errata: **none**

CURSED TOTEM
Versions: MI, 6E: R
Current Errata: **none**

D'AVENANT ARCHER
Versions: LE, CH, 5E, 6E:C
Current Errata: **none**

DANCING SCIMITAR
Versions: AN: U, RV, 4E, 5E, 6E: R
Current Errata: **none**

DARAJA GRIFFIN
Versions: VI, 6E: U
Current Errata: **none**

DARING APPRENTICE
Versions: MI, 6E: R
Current Errata: **none**

DEFLECTION
Versions: IA, 5E, 6E: R
Current Errata: **none**

DENSE FOLIAGE
Versions: WE, 6E: R
Current Errata: **none**

DERELOR
Versions: FE: U, 5E, 6E: R
Current Errata: **none**

DESERTION
Versions: VI, 6E: R
Current Errata: **none**

DIMINISHING RETURNS
Versions: AL, 6E: R
Current Errata: **none**

DINGUS EGG
Versions: A, B, UL, RV, 4E, 5E, 6E: R
Current Errata: **none**

DISENCHANT
Versions: IA, TE, MI, US, A, B, UL, RV, 4E, 5E, 6E: C
Current Errata: **none**

DISRUPTING SCEPTER
Versions: A, B, UL, RV, 4E, 5E, 6E: R
Current Errata: **none**

DIVINE TRANSFORMATION
Versions: LE, 4E, 5E, 6E: U
Current Errata: **none**

DOOMSDAY
Versions: WE, 6E: R
Current Errata: **none**

DRAGON ENGINE
Versions: AQ: C, A, B, UL, RV, 4E, 5E, 6E: R
Current Errata: **none**

DRAGON MASK
Versions: VI, 6E: U
Current Errata: **none**

DREAD OF NIGHT
Versions: TE, 6E: U
Current Errata: **none**

DREAM CACHE
Versions: TE, MI, 6E: C
Current Errata: **none**

DRUDGE SKELETONS
Versions: A, B, UL, RV, 4E, 5E, 6E: C
Current Errata: **none**

DRY SPELL
Versions: HM, 6E: C
Current Errata: **none**

DWARVEN RUINS
Versions: FE, 5E, 6E: U
Current Errata: **none**

EARLY HARVEST
Versions: MI, 6E: R
Current Errata: **none**

EARTHQUAKE
Versions: A, B, UL, RV, 4E, 5E, 6E: R
Current Errata: **none**

EBON STRONGHOLD
Versions: FE, 5E, 6E: U
Current Errata: **none**

EKUNDU GRIFFIN
Versions: MI, 6E: C
Current Errata: **none**

ELDER DRUID
Versions: IA, 5E, 6E: R
Current Errata: **none**

ELVEN CACHE
Versions: VI, 6E: C
Current Errata: **none**

ELVEN RIDERS
Versions: LG: R, 4E, 5E, 6E: U
Current Errata: **none**

ELVISH ARCHERS
Versions: A, B, UL, RV, 4E, 5E, 6E: R
Current Errata: **none**

ENFEEBLEMENT
Versions: MI, TE, 6E: C
Current Errata: **none**

ENLIGHTENED TUTOR
Versions: MI, 6E: U
Current Errata: **none**

ETHEREAL CHAMPION
Versions: MI, 6E: R
Current Errata: **none**

EVIL EYE OF ORMS-BY-GORE
Versions: LG, 5E, 6E: U
Current Errata: **none**

EXILE
Versions: AL, 6E: R
Current Errata: **none**

FALLEN ANGEL
Versions: LG, CH, 5E, 6E: R
Current Errata: **none**

FALLOW EARTH
Versions: MI, 6E: U
Current Errata: **none**

FAMILIAR GROUND
Versions: WE, 6E: U
Current Errata: **none**

FATAL BLOW
Versions: WE, 6E: C
Current Errata: **none**

FEAR
Versions: IA, A, B, UL, RV, 4E, 5E, 6E: C
Current Errata: **none**

FEAST OF THE UNICORN
Versions: HM, 6E: C
Current Errata: **none**

FEMEREF ARCHERS
Versions: MI, 6E: U
Current Errata: **none**

FERAL SHADOW
Versions: MI, 6E: C
Current Errata: **none**

FERVOR
Versions: WE, 6E: R
Current Errata: **none**

FINAL FORTUNE
Versions: MI, 6E: R
Current Errata: **none**

FIRE DIAMOND
Versions: MI, 6E: U
Current Errata: **none**

FIRE ELEMENTAL
Versions: A, B, UL, RV, 4E, 6E: U
Current Errata: **none**

FIREBREATHING
Versions: MI, A, B, UL, RV, 4E, 5E, 6E: C
Current Errata: **none**

FIT OF RAGE
Versions: WE, 6E: C
Current Errata: **none**

FLAME SPIRIT
Versions: IA, 5E: U, 6E: C
Current Errata: **none**

FLASH
Versions: MI, 6E: R
Current Errata: **none**

FLASHFIRES
Versions: A, B, UL, RV, 4E, 5E, 6E: U
Current Errata: **none**

FLIGHT
Versions: A, B, UL, RV, 4E, 5E, 6E: C
Current Errata: **none**

FLYING CARPET
Versions: AN, RV, 4E, 5E, 6E: R
Current Errata: **none**

FOG
Versions: MI, A, B, UL, RV, 4E, 5E, 6E: C
Current Errata: **none**

FOG ELEMENTAL
Versions: WE, 6E:C
Current Errata: **none**

FORBIDDEN CRYPT
Versions: MI, 6E: R
Current Errata: **none**

FOREST
Versions: 6E:L
Current Errata: **none**

FOREST
Versions: 6E:L
Current Errata: **none**

FOREST
Versions: 6E:L
Current Errata: **none**

FOREST
Versions: 6E:L
Current Errata: **none**

FORGET
Versions: HL, 5E, 6E: R
Current Errata: **none**

FOUNTAIN OF YOUTH
Versions: DK, CH, 5E, 6E: U
Current Errata: **none**

FYNDHORN BROWNIE
Versions: IA, 6E: C
Current Errata: **none**

FYNDHORN ELDER
Versions: IA, 5E, 6E: U
Current Errata: **none**

GASEOUS FORM
Versions: LG, TE, 4E, 5E, 6E: C
Current Errata: **none**

GIANT GROWTH
Versions: IA, A, B, UL, RV, 4E, 5E, 6E: C
Current Errata: **none**

GIANT SPIDER
Versions: A, B, UL, RV, 4E, 5E, 6E: C
Current Errata: **none**

GIANT STRENGTH
Versions: LG, TE, 4E, 5E, 6E: C
Current Errata: **none**

GLACIAL WALL
Versions: IA, 5E, 6E: U
Current Errata: **none**

GLASSES OF URZA
Versions: A, B, UL, RV, 4E, 5E, 6E: U
Current Errata: **none**

GOBLIN DIGGING TEAM
Versions: DK, CH, 5E, 6E: C
Current Errata: **none**

GOBLIN ELITE INFANTRY
Versions: MI, 6E: C
Current Errata: **none**

GOBLIN HERO
Versions: DK, 5E, 6E: C
Current Errata: **none**

GOBLIN KING
Versions: A, B, UL, RV, 4E, 5E, 6E: R
Current Errata: **none**

GOBLIN RECRUITER
Versions: VI, 6E: U
Current Errata: **none**

GOBLIN WARRENS
Versions: FE, 5E, 6E: R
Current Errata: **none**

GORILLA CHEIFTAIN
Versions: AL, 6E: C
Current Errata: **none**

GRAVEBANE ZOMBIE
Versions: MI: C, 6E: U
Current Errata: **none**

GRAVEDIGGER
Versions: TE, 6E: C
Current Errata: **none**

GREED
Versions: LG, 4E, 6E: R
Current Errata: **none**

GRINNING TOTEM
Versions: MI, 6E: R
Current Errata: **none**

GRIZZLY BEARS
Versions: A, B, UL, RV, 4E, 5E, 6E: C
Current Errata: **none**

HAMMER OF BOGARDAN
Versions: MI, 6E: R
Current Errata: **none**

HARMATTAN EFREET
Versions: MI, 6E: U
Current Errata: **none**

HAVENWOOD BATTLEGROUND
Versions: FE, 5E, 6E: U
Current Errata: **none**

HEALING SALVE
Versions: US, A, B, UL, RV, 4E, 5E, 6E: C
Current Errata: **none**

HEAVY BALLISTA
Versions: WE, 6E: U
Current Errata: **none**

HECATOMB
Versions: IA, 5E, 6E: R
Current Errata: **none**

HERO'S RESOLVE
Versions: TE, 6E: C
Current Errata: **none**

HIDDEN HORROR
Versions: WE, 6E: U
Current Errata: **none**

HORNED TURTLE
Versions: TE, 6E: C
Current Errata: **none**

HOWL FROM BEYOND
Versions: IA, A, B, UL, RV, 4E, 5E, 6E: C
Current Errata: **none**

HOWLING MINE
Versions: A, B, UL, RV, 4E, 5E, 6E: R
Current Errata: **none**

HULKING CYCLOPS
Versions: VI, 6E: U
Current Errata: **none**

HURRICANE
Versions: IA, A, B, UL, RV, 4E, 5E, 6E: R
Current Errata: **none**

ICATIAN TOWN
Versions: FE, 5E, 6E: R
Current Errata: **none**

ILLICIT AUCTION
Versions: MI, 6E: R
Current Errata: **none**

INFANTRY VETERAN
Versions: VI, 6E: C
Current Errata: **none**

INFERNAL CONTRACT
Versions: MI, 6E: R
Current Errata: **none**

INFERNO
Versions: DK, 4E, 5E, 6E: R
Current Errata: **none**

INSIGHT
Versions: TE, 6E: U
Current Errata: **none**

INSPIRATION
Versions: VI, 6E: C
Current Errata: **none**

IRON STAR
Versions: A, B, UL, RV, 4E, 5E, 6E: U
Current Errata: **none**

ISLAND
Versions: 6E:L
Current Errata: **none**

ISLAND
Versions: 6E:L
Current Errata: **none**

ISLAND
Versions: 6E:L
Current Errata: **none**

ISLAND
Versions: 6E:L
Current Errata: **none**

IVORY CUP
Versions: A, B, UL, RV, 4E, 5E, 6E: U
Current Errata: **none**

JADE MONOLITH
Versions: A, B, UL, RV, 4E, 5E, 6E: R
Current Errata: **none**

JALUM TOME
Versions: AQ, CH, 5E, 6E: R
Current Errata: **none**

JAYEMDAE TOME
Versions: A, B, UL, RV, 4E, 5E, 6E: R
Current Errata: **none**

JOKULHAUPS
Versions: IA, 5E, 6E: R
Current Errata: **none**

JUXTAPOSE
Versions: LG, CH, 5E, 6E: R
Current Errata: **none**

KARPLUSAN FOREST
Versions: IA, 5E, 6E: R
Current Errata: **none**

KISMET
Versions: LE, 4E, 5E, 6E: U
Current Errata: **none**

KJELDORAN DEAD
Versions: IA, 5E, 6E: C
Current Errata: **none**

KJELDORAN ROYAL GUARD
Versions: IA, 5E, 6E: R
Current Errata: **none**

LEAD GOLEM
Versions: MI, 6E: U
Current Errata: **none**

LESHRAC'S RITE
Versions: IA, 5E, 6E: U
Current Errata: **none**

LIBRARY OF LAT-NAM
Versions: AL, 6E: R
Current Errata: **none**

LIGHT OF DAY
Versions: TE, 6E: U
Current Errata: **none**

LIGHTNING BLAST
Versions: TE, 6E: C
Current Errata: **none**

LIVING LANDS
Versions: A, B, UL, RV, 4E, 5E, 6E: R
Current Errata: **none**

LLANOWAR ELVES
Versions: A, B, UL, RV, 4E, 5E, 6E: C
Current Errata: **none**

LONGBOW ARCHER
Versions: VI, 6E: U
Current Errata: **none**

LORD OF ATLANTIS
Versions: A, B, UL, RV, 4E, 5E, 6E: R
Current Errata: **none**

LOST SOUL
Versions: LG, 4E, 5E, 6E: C
Current Errata: **none**

LURE
Versions: IA, 5E, 6E: U
Current Errata: **none**

MANA PRISM
Versions: MI, 6E: U
Current Errata: **none**

MANA SHORT
Versions: A, B, UL, RV, 4E, 6E: R
Current Errata: **none**

MANABARBS
Versions: A, B, UL, RV, 4E, 5E, 6E: R
Current Errata: **none**

MARBLE DIAMOND
Versions: MI, 6E: U
Current Errata: **none**

MARO
Versions: MI, 6E: R
Current Errata: **none**

MEEKSTONE
Versions: A, B, UL, RV, 4E, 5E, 6E: R
Current Errata: **none**

MEMORY LAPSE
Versions: HM, MI, 5E, 6E: C
Current Errata: **none**

MERFOLK OF THE PEARL TRIDENT
Versions: A, B, UL, RV, 4E, 5E, 6E: C
Current Errata: **none**

MESA FALCON
Versions: HM, 5E, 6E: C
Current Errata: **none**

MILLSTONE
Versions: AQ: U, RV, 4E, 5E, 6E: R
Current Errata: **none**

MIND WARP
Versions: IA, 5E, 6E: U
Current Errata: **none**

MISCHIEVOUS POLTERGIEST
Versions: WE, 6E: U
Current Errata: **none**

MOSS DIAMOND
Versions: MI, 6E: U
Current Errata: **none**

MOUNTAIN
Versions: 6E:L
Current Errata: **none**

MOUNTAIN
Versions: 6E:L
Current Errata: **none**

MOUNTAIN
Versions: 6E:L
Current Errata: **none**

MOUNTAIN
Versions: 6E:L
Current Errata: **none**

MOUNTAIN GOAT
Versions: IA, 5E, 6E: C
Current Errata: **none**

MYSTIC COMPASS
Versions: AL, 6E: U
Current Errata: **none**

MYSTICAL TUTOR
Versions: **MI, 6E: U**
Current Errata: **none**

NATURE'S RESURGENCE
Versions: **WE, 6E: R**
Current Errata: **none**

NECROSAVANT
Versions: **VI, 6E: R**
Current Errata: **none**

NIGHTMARE
Versions: **A, B, UL, RV, 4E, 5E, 6E: R**
Current Errata: **none**

OBSIANUS GOLEM
Versions: **A, B, UL, RV, 4E, 6E: U**
Current Errata: **none**

ORCISH ARTILLERY
Versions: **A, B, UL, RV, 4E, 5E, 6E: U**
Current Errata: **none**

ORCISH ORIFLAMME
Versions: **A, B, UL, RV, 4E, 5E, 6E: U**
Current Errata: **none**

ORDER OF THE SACRED TORCH
Versions: **IA, 5E, 6E: R**
Current Errata: **none**

ORNITHOPTER
Versions: **AQ, RV, 4E, 5E, 6E: U**
Current Errata: **none**

PACIFISM
Versions: **MI, TE, US, 6E: C**
Current Errata: **none**

PAINFUL MEMORIES
Versions: **MI, 6E: C**
Current Errata: **none**

PANTHER WARRIORS
Versions: **VI, 6E: C**
Current Errata: **none**

PATAGIA GOLEM
Versions: MI, 6E: U
Current Errata: **none**

PEARL DRAGON
Versions: MI, 6E: R
Current Errata: **none**

PENTAGRAM OF THE AGES
Versions: IA, 5E, 6E: R
Current Errata: **none**

PERISH
Versions: TE, 6E: U
Current Errata: **none**

PESTILENCE
Versions: US, A, B, UL, RV, 4E, 5E, 6E: U
Current Errata: **none**

PHANTASMAL TERRAIN
Versions: A, B, UL, RV, 4E, 5E, 6E: C
Current Errata: **none**

PHANTOM WARRIOR
Versions: WE, 6E: U
Current Errata: **none**

PHYREXIAN VAULT
Versions: MI, 6E: U
Current Errata: **none**

PILLAGE
Versions: AL, 6E: U
Current Errata: **none**

PLAINS
Versions: 6E:L
Current Errata: **none**

PLAINS
Versions: 6E:L
Current Errata: **none**

PLAINS
Versions: 6E:L
Current Errata: **none**

PLAINS
Versions: 6E:L
Current Errata: none

POLYMORPH
Versions: MI, 6E: R
Current Errata: none

POWER SINK
Versions: IA, TE, MI, US, A, B, UL, RV, 4E, 5E, 6E: U
Current Errata: none

PRADESH GYPSIES
Versions: LG, 4E, 5E, 6E: C
Current Errata: none

PRIMAL CLAY
Versions: AQ, RV, 4E, 5E, 6E: R
Current Errata: none

PRODIGAL SORCERER
Versions: A, B, UL, RV, 4E, 5E, 6E: C
Current Errata: none

PROSPERITY
Versions: VI, 6E: U
Current Errata: none

PSYCHIC TRANSFER
Versions: MI, 6E: R
Current Errata: none

PSYCHIC VENOM
Versions: A, B, UL, RV, 4E, 5E, 6E: C
Current Errata: none

PYROTECHNICS
Versions: LG:C2, 4E, 5E, 6E: C
Current Errata: none

PYTHON
Versions: VI, 6E: C
Current Errata: none

RADJAN SPIRIT
Versions: LG, 4E, 5E, 6E: U
Current Errata: none

RAG MAN
Versions: DK, 4E, 5E, 6E: R
Current Errata: **none**

RAGING GOBLIN
Versions: EX, 6E: C
Current Errata: **none**

RAISE DEAD
Versions: A, B, UL, RV, 4E, 5E, 6E: C
Current Errata: **none**

RAMPANT GROWTH
Versions: MI, TE, 6E: C
Current Errata: **none**

RAZORTOOTH RATS
Versions: WE, 6E: C
Current Errata: **none**

RECALL
Versions: LG, CH: U3, 5E, 6E: R
Current Errata: **none**

RECKLESS EMBERMAGE
Versions: MI, 6E: R
Current Errata: **none**

REDWOOD TREEFOLK
Versions: WE, 6E: C
Current Errata: **none**

REGAL UNICORN
Versions: PO, 6E:C
Current Errata: **none**

REGENERATION
Versions: IA, MI, A, B, UL, RV, 4E, 5E, 6E: C
Current Errata: **none**

RELEARN
Versions: WE, 6E: U
Current Errata: **none**

RELENTLESS ASSAULT
Versions: VI, 6E: R
Current Errata: **none**

REMEDY
Versions: VI, 6E: C
Current Errata: none

REMOVE SOUL
Versions: LG: C2, CH: C3, 5E, 6E: C
Current Errata: none

REPRISAL
Versions: AL, 6E: U
Current Errata: none

RESISTANCE FIGHTER
Versions: VI, 6E: C
Current Errata: none

REVERSE DAMAGE
Versions: A, B, UL, RV, 4E, 5E, 6E: R
Current Errata: none

RIVER BOA
Versions: VI, 6E: U
Current Errata: none

ROD OF RUIN
Versions: A, B, UL, RV, 4E, 5E, 6E: U
Current Errata: none

ROWEN
Versions: VI, 6E: R
Current Errata: none

RUINS OF TROKAIR
Versions: FE: U2, 5E, 6E: U
Current Errata: none

SABRETOOTH TIGER
Versions: IA, 5E, 6E: C
Current Errata: none

SAGE OWL
Versions: WE, 6E: C
Current Errata: none

SAMITE HEALER
Versions: A, B, UL, RV, 4E, 5E, 6E: C
Current Errata: none

SCALED WURM
Versions: IA, 5E, 6E: C
Current Errata: **none**

SCALED ZOMBIES
Versions: A, B, UL, RV, 4E, 5E, 6E: C
Current Errata: **none**

SEA MONSTER
Versions: TE, 6E: C
Current Errata: **none**

SEGOVIAN LEVIATHAN
Versions: LG:U1, 4E, 5E, 6E: U
Current Errata: **none**

SENGIR AUTOCRAT
Versions: HL:U1, 5E, 6E: R
Current Errata: **none**

SERENITY
Versions: WE, 6E: R
Current Errata: **none**

SERRA'S BLESSING
Versions: WE, 6E: U
Current Errata: **none**

SHANODIN DRYADS
Versions: A, B, UL, RV, 4E, 5E, 6E: C
Current Errata: **none**

SHATTER
Versions: IA, TE, A, B, UL, RV, 4E, 5E, 6E: C
Current Errata: **none**

SHATTERSTORM
Versions: AQ: U1, A, B, UL, RV, 5E, 6E: R
Current Errata: **none**

SHOCK
Versions: ST, 6E: C
Current Errata: **none**

SIBILANT SPIRIT
Versions: IA, 5E, 6E: R
Current Errata: **none**

SKULL CATAPULT
Versions: 1A, 5E, 6E: U
Current Errata: **none**

SKY DIAMOND
Versions: MI, 6E: U
Current Errata: **none**

SNAKE BASKET
Versions: VI, 6E: R
Current Errata: **none**

SOLDEVI SAGE
Versions: AL, 6E: U
Current Errata: **none**

SOUL NET
Versions: A, B, UL, RV, 4E, 5E, 6E: U
Current Errata: **none**

SPELL BLAST
Versions: TE, A, B, UL, RV, 4E, 5E, 6E: C
Current Errata: **none**

SPIRIT LINK
Versions: LG: U1, 4E, 5E, 6E: U
Current Errata: **none**

SPITTING DRAKE
Versions: VI, 6E: U
Current Errata: **none**

SPITTING EARTH
Versions: MI, 6E: C
Current Errata: **none**

STALKING TIGER
Versions: MI, 6E: C
Current Errata: **none**

STANDING TROOPS
Versions: EX, 6E: C
Current Errata: **none**

STAUNCH DEFENDERS
Versions: TE, 6E: U
Current Errata: **none**

STONE RAIN
Versions: IA, MI, TE, A, B, UL, RV, 4E, 5E, 6E: C
Current Errata: **none**

STORM CAULDRON
Versions: AL, 6E: R
Current Errata: **none**

STORM CROW
Versions: AL:C3, 6E: C
Current Errata: **none**

STRANDS OF NIGHT
Versions: WE, 6E: U
Current Errata: **none**

STREAM OF LIFE
Versions: A, B, UL, RV, 4E, 5E, 6E: C
Current Errata: **none**

STROMGALD CABAL
Versions: IA, 5E, 6E: R
Current Errata: **none**

STUPOR
Versions: MI, 6E: U
Current Errata: **none**

SULFUROUS SPRINGS
Versions: IA, 5E, 6E: R
Current Errata: **none**

SUMMER BLOOM
Versions: VI, 6E: U
Current Errata: **none**

SUNWEB
Versions: MI, 6E: R
Current Errata: **none**

SVEYELUNITE TEMPLE
Versions: FE:U2, 5E, 6E: U
Current Errata: **none**

SWAMP
Versions: 6E:L
Current Errata: **none**

SWAMP
Versions: 6E:L
Current Errata: **none**

SWAMP
Versions: 6E:L
Current Errata: **none**

SWAMP
Versions: 6E:L
Current Errata: **none**

SYPHON SOUL
Versions: LG:C2, 6E: C
Current Errata: **none**

TALRUUM MINOTAUR
Versions: MI, 6E: C
Current Errata: **none**

TARIFF
Versions: WE, 6E: R
Current Errata: **none**

TEFERI'S PUZZLE BOX
Versions: VI, 6E: R
Current Errata: **none**

TERROR
Versions: A, B, UL, RV, 4E, 5E, 6E: C
Current Errata: **none**

THE HIVE
Versions: A, B, UL, RV, 4E, 5E, 6E: R
Current Errata: **none**

THICKET BASILISK
Versions: A, B, UL, RV, 4E, 5E, 6E: U
Current Errata: **none**

THRONE OF BONE
Versions: A, B, UL, RV, 4E, 5E, 6E: U
Current Errata: **none**

TIDAL SURGE
Versions: ST, 6E: C
Current Errata: **none**

TRAINED ARMODON
Versions: TE, 6E: C
Current Errata: **none**

TRANQUIL GROVE
Versions: WE, 6E: R
Current Errata: **none**

TRANQUILITY
Versions: TE, A, B, UL, RV, 4E, 5E, 6E: C
Current Errata: **none**

TREMOR
Versions: VI, 6E: C
Current Errata: **none**

TUNDRA WOLVES
Versions: LG:C2, 4E, 5E, 6E: C
Current Errata: **none**

UKTABI ORANGUTAN
Versions: VI, 6E: U
Current Errata: **none**

UKTABI WILDCATS
Versions: MI, 6E: R
Current Errata: **none**

UNDERGROUND RIVER
Versions: IA, 5E: R
Current Errata: **none**

UNSEEN WALKER
Versions: MI, 6E: U
Current Errata: **none**

UNSUMMON
Versions: A, B, UL, RV, 4E, 5E, 6E: C
Current Errata: **none**

UNTAMED WILDS
Versions: LG:U1, 4E, 5E, 6E: U
Current Errata: **none**

UNYARO GRIFFIN
Versions: MI, 6E: U
Current Errata: **none**

VAMPIRIC TUTOR
Versions: **VI, 6E: R**
Current Errata: **none**

VENERABLE MONK
Versions: **ST, 6E: C**
Current Errata: **none**

VERDURAN ENCHANTRESS
Versions: **A, B, UL, RV, 4E, 5E, 6E: R**
Current Errata: **none**

VERTIGO
Versions: **IA, 6E: U**
Current Errata: **none**

VIASHINO WARRIOR
Versions: **MI, 6E: C**
Current Errata: **none**

VITALIZE
Versions: **WE, 6E: C**
Current Errata: **none**

VODALIAN SOLDIERS
Versions: **FE, 5E, 6E: C**
Current Errata: **none**

VOLCANIC DRAGON
Versions: **MI, 6E: R**
Current Errata: **none**

VOLCANIC GEYSER
Versions: **MI, 6E: U**
Current Errata: **none**

WAITING IN THE WEEDS
Versions: **MI, 6E: R**
Current Errata: **none**

WALL OF AIR
Versions: **A, B, UL, RV, 4E, 5E, 6E: U**
Current Errata: **none**

WALL OF FIRE
Versions: **A, B, UL, RV, 4E, 5E, 6E: U**
Current Errata: **none**

WALL OF SWORDS
Versions: A, B, UL, RV, 4E, 5E, 6E: U
Current Errata: **none**

WAND OF DENIAL
Versions: VI, 6E: R
Current Errata: **none**

WARMTH
Versions: TE, 6E: U
Current Errata: **none**

WARRIOR'S HONOR
Versions: VI:C, 6E: C
Current Errata: **none**

WARTHOG
Versions: VI:C, 6E: U
Current Errata: **none**

WILD GROWTH
Versions: IA, A, B, UL, RV, 4E, 5E, 6E: C
Current Errata: **none**

WIND DRAKE
Versions: TE, 6E: C
Current Errata: **none**

WIND SPIRIT
Versions: IA, 5E, 6E: U
Current Errata: **none**

WOODEN SPHERE
Versions: A, B, UL, RV, 4E, 5E, 6E: U
Current Errata: **none**

WORLDLY TUTOR
Versions: MI, 5E: U
Current Errata: **none**

WRATH OF GOD
Versions: A, B, UL, RV, 4E, 5E, 6E: R
Current Errata: **none**

WYLULI WOLF
Versions: AN:C4, 5E, 6E: R
Current Errata: **none**

ZOMBIE MASTER
Versions: **A, B, UL, RV, 4E, 5E, 6E: R**
Current Errata: **none**

ZUR'S WEIRDING
Versions: **IA, 5E, 6E: R**
Current Errata: **none**

OVERVIEW

The *Urza's Destiny*™ expansion completes the Urza trilogy. From a story standpoint, it finishes the flashback begun in the *Urza's Saga* set by filling in the rest of the events leading to Gerrard's childhood. On the card mechanics side, the *Urza's Destiny* set is less closely linked to the other two Urza-cycle sets. It makes some use of the abilities introduced with *Urza's Saga* and *Urza's Legacy* cards, but it has a very strong flavor of its own and introduces two brand new themes.

This expansion includes five creatures with echo and three cards with cycling. Unlike the *Urza's Saga* and *Urza's Legacy* cards, these cards don't have reminder text defining the abilities—you need a rules sheet to tell you what it means. The "sleeping enchantment" and "free spell" mechanics received only one token card apiece. However, the "growing enchantments" theme from the *Urza's Saga* set, which was absent from the *Urza's Legacy* expansion, was reintroduced with a twist. This set has five "growing" enchant creature cards. These enchantments provide an ever-increasing effect for the enchanted creature.

The new *Urza's Destiny* themes are the "reveal" and "lobotomy" cycles. The "reveal" cards come in two types: creatures (Seers) and spells (Scents). Every color received one of each. When you use a Seer ability or a Scent spell, you show your oppo-nents any number of cards of the specified color that are currently in your hand. The number of cards revealed determines the power of the effect.

The "lobotomy" cards gain their nickname from the *Tempest* spell Lobotomy, which allowed you to look at a player's hand, choose a card, and remove all copies of that card from his or her hand, graveyard, and library. The *Urza's Destiny* set gives each color a specialized version of this effect. The blue one, Quash, counters an instant or sorcery and removes all copies of it; the other four target something that's already in play and remove both it and any other copies in hand, graveyard, or library. (They don't remove others that are already in play.)

The *Urza's Destiny* expansion also has a strong theme of graveyard effects. Many creatures and a few enchantments have special abilities that trigger when the permanent is put into a graveyard. These cards encourage combinations with spells and abilities that destroy or sacrifice your own creatures or that return things from your graveyard for re-use.

KEY CARDS

Yawgmoth's Bargain. Widely regarded by players as the most "broken" card in the set, this card is quite likely to be banned from some forms of DCI tournament play before this encyclopedia sees print. Like the old enchantment Necropotence, this card allows a player to trade life for cards on a one-for-one basis. But the Bargain lets you do this at any time, one card at a time, rather than paying up front and getting all the cards at the end of your turn.

Replenish. This white sorcery gives you a way to get all your expensive enchantments into play for free. You just have to get them into the graveyard first—and there are plenty of ways to do that. It's a key ingredient for many combo decks.

Opalescence. A rules guru's nightmare: this enchantment causes great confusion when combined with anything that removes abilities from creatures, and it's strong enough to be used in a number of tournament decks.

Masticore. A big, buff 4/4 creature for only four mana that also provides reusable direct damage. All this, and it regenerates, too! Get one of these into play early enough, and you won't mind having to discard a card every turn.

Eradicate. Of all the "lobotomy" spells, this one caused the biggest uproar. Combine it with a spell that turns lands into creatures (such as the *Stronghold*™ instant Verdant Touch) and you can strip all the land of one type out of your opponent's deck.

Treachery. A "free" Control Magic for only one more mana than the original version.

Plow Under. Green control decks are somewhat rare—often, green strategy consists of just overrunning your opponent with a creature horde. Plow Under, however, is a premium card for green control. Against many decks it acts as a two-turn Time Walk.

Caltrops. This card is good by itself against weenie decks and is often used in combination with Humility to completely shut down creature attacks.

THE STORY

The *Urza's Destiny* story covers the final element in Urza's grand design for defeating the Pyrexian invasion: his creation of an "organic component" to wield the Legacy.

From ancient Thran records, Urza learns techniques for manipulating evolution. He begins applying these to various Dominarian humans. He also begins construction of an army of magical soldiers called Metathran. Many of his Tolarian allies are horrified when they learn of these manipulations, and some resign from the academy. One, though—the tutor Gatha—tries to copy Urza's methods, using the warrior nation of Keld as his test subjects. His experiments eventually produce even fiercer Keldon warlords. Finally Gatha's manipulations draw the attention of the Phyrexians, so Urza shuts them down. While he is doing so, a pack of Phyrexian negators that has been on his track for centuries catches up with him. Urza destroys all but one and chases that one through a portal before finally defeating it.

Meanwhile, the elf Rofellos is sent as an ambassador from Llanowar to Yavimaya. He becomes good friends with Multani, the Maro-sorcerer of Yavimaya, and witnesses the evolution of the forest as Yavimaya makes its own preparations for the invasion. A band of Phyrexians attacks the forest and is destroyed by the elves and forest creatures, many of whom have been bred into fearsome monsters.

After destroying the last negator, Urza investigates this plane, which turns out to be Rath. It's ruled by the self-proclaimed evincar Davvol and forms a key part of the Phyrexian invasion plans. While exploring, Urza encounters the Soltari and makes an agreement with Lyna, their emissary: he will help her people escape the shadow world they're trapped in if they will aid in the invasion defense. He then returns to Dominaria to complete his work on the Legacy's organic component.

Back on Dominaria, the Phyrexians have discovered Urza's bloodline manipulations and begin to attack these regions. The silver golem Karn manages to save the last survivor of one of these bloodlines, the Capashen clan, after the Phyrexians destroy an entire village. He takes this sole survivor to Jamuraa. The child's name should be familiar to those who followed the *Weatherlight*™ and Rath sagas: it is Gerrard.

ACADEMY RECTOR
Versions: UD:R
Current Errata: **none**

ÆTHER STING
Versions: UD:U
Current Errata: **none**

ANCIENT SILVERBACK
Versions: UD:R
Current Errata: **none**

APPRENTICE NECROMANCER
Versions: UD:R
Current Errata: **none**

ARCHERY TRAINING
Versions: UD:U
Current Errata: **none**

ATTRITION
Versions: UD:R
Current Errata: **none**

AURA THIEF
Versions: UD:R
Current Errata: **none**

BLIZZARD ELEMENTAL
Versions: UD:R
Current Errata: **none**

BLOODSHOT CYCLOPS
Versions: UD:R
Current Errata: **none**

BODY SNATCHER
Versions: UD:R
Current Errata: **none**

BRAIDWOOD CUP
Versions: UD:U
Current Errata: **none**

BRAIDWOOD SEXTANT
Versions: UD:R
Current Errata: **none**

BRASS SECRETARY
Versions: **UD:U**
Current Errata: **none**

BRINE SEER
Versions: **UD:U**
Current Errata: **none**

BUBBLING BEEBLES
Versions: **UD:C**
Current Errata: **none**

BUBBLING MUCK
Versions: **UD:C**
Current Errata: **none**

CALTROPS
Versions: **UD:U**
Current Errata: **none**

CAPASHEN KNIGHT
Versions: **UD:C**
Current Errata: **none**

CAPASHEN STANDARD
Versions: **UD:C**
Current Errata: **none**

CAPASHEN TEMPLAR
Versions: **UD:C**
Current Errata: **none**

CARNIVAL OF SOULS
Versions: **UD:R**
Current Errata: **none**

CHIME OF NIGHT
Versions: **UD:C**
Current Errata: **none**

CINDER SEER
Versions: **UD:U**
Current Errata: **none**

COLOS YEARLING
Versions: **UD:C**
Current Errata: **none**

COMPOST
Versions: **UD:C**
Current Errata: **none**

COVETOUS DRAGON
Versions: **UD:R**
Current Errata: **none**

DISAPPEAR
Versions: **UD:U**
Current Errata: **none**

DISEASE CARRIERS
Versions: **UD:C**
Current Errata: **none**

DONATE
Versions: **UD:R**
Current Errata: **none**

DYING WAIL
Versions: **UD:C**
Current Errata: **none**

ELVISH LOOKOUT
Versions: **UD:C**
Current Errata: **none**

ELVISH PIPER
Versions: **UD:R**
Current Errata: **none**

EMPEROR CROCODILE
Versions: **UD:R**
Current Errata: **none**

ENCROACH
Versions: **UD:U**
Current Errata: **none**

ERADICATE
Versions: **UD:U**
Current Errata: **none**

EXTRUDER
Versions: **UD:U**
Current Errata: **none**

FALSE PROPHET
Versions: **UD:R**
Current Errata: **none**

FATIGUE
Versions: **UD:C**
Current Errata: **none**

FEND OFF
Versions: **UD:C**
Current Errata: **none**

FESTERING WOUND
Versions: **UD:U**
Current Errata: **none**

FIELD SURGEON
Versions: **UD:C**
Current Errata: **none**

FLAME JET
Versions: **UD:C**
Current Errata: **none**

FLEDGLING OSPREY
Versions: **UD:C**
Current Errata: **none**

FLICKER
Versions: **UD:R**
Current Errata: **none**

FODDER CANNON
Versions: **UD:U**
Current Errata: **none**

GAMEKEEPER
Versions: **UD:U**
Current Errata: **none**

GOBLIN BERSERKER
Versions: **UD:U**
Current Errata: **none**

GOBLIN FESTIVAL
Versions: **UD:R**
Current Errata: **none**

GOBLIN GARDENER
Versions: **UD:C**
Current Errata: **none**

GOBLIN MARSHAL
Versions: **UD:R**
Current Errata: **none**

GOBLIN MASONS
Versions: **UD:C**
Current Errata: **none**

GOLIATH BEETLE
Versions: **UD:C**
Current Errata: **none**

HEART WARDEN
Versions: **UD:C**
Current Errata: **none**

HULKING OGRE
Versions: **UD:C**
Current Errata: **none**

HUNTING MOA
Versions: **UD:U**
Current Errata: **none**

ILLUMINATED WINGS
Versions: **UD:C**
Current Errata: **none**

IMPATIENCE
Versions: **UD:R**
Current Errata: **none**

INCENDIARY
Versions: **UD:U**
Current Errata: **none**

IRIDESCENT DRAKE
Versions: **UD:U**
Current Errata: **none**

IVY SEER
Versions: **UD:U**
Current Errata: **none**

JASMINE SEER
Versions: **UD:U**
Current Errata: **none**

JUNK DIVER
Versions: **UD:R**
Current Errata: **none**

KELDON CHAMPION
Versions: **UD:U**
Current Errata: **none**

KELDON VANDALS
Versions: **UD:C**
Current Errata: **none**

KINGFISHER
Versions: **UD:C**
Current Errata: **none**

LANDSLIDE
Versions: **UD:U**
Current Errata: **none**

LURKING JACKALS
Versions: **UD:U**
Current Errata: **none**

MAGNIFY
Versions: **UD:C**
Current Errata: **none**

MANTIS ENGINE
Versions: **UD:U**
Current Errata: **none**

MARK OF FURY
Versions: **UD:C**
Current Errata: **none**

MARKER BEETLES
Versions: **UD:C**
Current Errata: **none**

MASK OF LAW AND GRACE
Versions: **UD:C**
Current Errata: **none**

MASTER HEALER
Versions: **UD:R**
Current Errata: **none**

MASTICORE
Versions: **UD:R**
Current Errata: **none**

MENTAL DISCIPLINE
Versions: **UD:C**
Current Errata: **none**

METALWORKER
Versions: **UD:R**
Current Errata: **none**

METATHRAN ELITE
Versions: **UD:U**
Current Errata: **none**

METATHRAN SOLDIER
Versions: **UD:C**
Current Errata: **none**

MOMENTUM
Versions: **UD:U**
Current Errata: **none**

MULTANI'S DECREE
Versions: **UD:C**
Current Errata: **none**

NIGHTSHADE SEER
Versions: **UD:U**
Current Errata: **none**

OPALESCENCE
Versions: **UD:R**
Current Errata: **none**

OPPOSITION
Versions: **UD:R**
Current Errata: **none**

PATTERN OF REBIRTH
Versions: **UD:R**
Current Errata: **none**

PHYREXIAN MONITOR
Versions: **UD:C**
Current Errata: **none**

PHYREXIAN NEGATOR
Versions: **UD:R**
Current Errata: **none**

PLAGUE DOGS
Versions: **UD:U**
Current Errata: **none**

PLATED SPIDER
Versions: **UD:C**
Current Errata: **none**

PLOW UNDER
Versions: **UD:R**
Current Errata: **none**

POWDER KEG
Versions: **UD:R**
Current Errata: **none**

PRIVATE RESEARCH
Versions: **UD:U**
Current Errata: **none**

QUASH
Versions: **UD:U**
Current Errata: **none**

RAPID DECAY
Versions: **UD:R**
Current Errata: **none**

RAVENOUS RATS
Versions: **UD:C**
Current Errata: **none**

RAYNE, ACADEMY CHANCELLOR
Versions: **UD:R**
Current Errata: **none**

RECKLESS ABANDON
Versions: **UD:C**
Current Errata: **none**

RELIQUARY MONK
Versions: UD:C
Current Errata: **none**

REPERCUSSION
Versions: UD:R
Current Errata: **none**

REPLENISH
Versions: UD:R
Current Errata: **none**

RESCUE
Versions: UD:C
Current Errata: **none**

ROFELLOS, LLANOWAR EMISSARY
Versions: UD:R
Current Errata: **none**

ROFELLOS'S GIFT
Versions: UD:C
Current Errata: **none**

SANCTIMONY
Versions: UD:U
Current Errata: **none**

SCENT OF BRINE
Versions: UD:C
Current Errata: **none**

SCENT OF CINDER
Versions: UD:C
Current Errata: **none**

SCENT OF IVY
Versions: UD:C
Current Errata: **none**

SCENT OF JASMINE
Versions: UD:C
Current Errata: **none**

SCENT OF NIGHTSHADE
Versions: UD:C
Current Errata: **none**

SCOUR
Versions: UD:U
Current Errata: none

SCRYING GLASS
Versions: UD:R
Current Errata: none

SERRA ADVOCATE
Versions: UD:U
Current Errata: none

SIGIL OF SLEEP
Versions: UD:C
Current Errata: none

SKITTERING HORROR
Versions: UD:C
Current Errata: none

SLINKING SKIRGE
Versions: UD:C
Current Errata: none

SOLIDARITY
Versions: UD:C
Current Errata: none

SOUL FEAST
Versions: UD:U
Current Errata: none

SOWING SALT
Versions: UD:U
Current Errata: none

SPLINTER
Versions: UD:U
Current Errata: none

SQUIRMING MASS
Versions: UD:C
Current Errata: none

STORAGE MATRIX
Versions: UD:R
Current Errata: none

TAUNTING ELF
Versions: **UD:C**
Current Errata: **none**

TELEPATHIC SPIES
Versions: **UD:C**
Current Errata: **none**

TEMPORAL ADEPT
Versions: **UD:R**
Current Errata: **none**

TETHERED GRIFFIN
Versions: **UD:R**
Current Errata: **none**

THIEVING MAGPIE
Versions: **UD:U**
Current Errata: **none**

THORN ELEMENTAL
Versions: **UD:R**
Current Errata: **none**

THRAN DYNAMO
Versions: **UD:U**
Current Errata: **none**

THRAN FOUNDRY
Versions: **UD:U**
Current Errata: **none**

THRAN GOLEM
Versions: **UD:R**
Current Errata: **none**

TORMENTED ANGEL
Versions: **UD:C**
Current Errata: **none**

TREACHERY
Versions: **UD:R**
Current Errata: **none**

TRUMPET BLAST
Versions: **UD:C**
Current Errata: **none**

TWISTED EXPERIMENT
Versions: **UD:C**
Current Errata: **none**

URZA'S INCUBATOR
Versions: **UD:R**
Current Errata: **none**

VOICE OF DUTY
Versions: **UD:U**
Current Errata: **none**

VOICE OF REASON
Versions: **UD:U**
Current Errata: **none**

WAKE OF DESTRUCTION
Versions: **UD:R**
Current Errata: **none**

WALL OF GLARE
Versions: **UD:C**
Current Errata: **none**

WILD COLOS
Versions: **UD:C**
Current Errata: **none**

YAVIMAYA ELDER
Versions: **UDC**
Current Errata: **none**

YAVIMAYA ENCHANTRESS
Versions: **UD:U**
Current Errata: **none**

YAVIMAYA HOLLOW
Versions: **UD:R**
Current Errata: **none**

YAWGMOTH'S BARGAIN
Versions: **UD:R**
Current Errata: **none**

PORTAL
Three Kingdoms ™

Overview

The *Portal Three Kingdoms*™ set is a special product that falls a bit outside the standard **Magic: The Gathering** family, though the cards are fully compatible with other **Magic** cards.

The story is based on a famous Chinese legend with some historical basis, as familiar in Asian countries as tales of King Arthur and the knights of Camelot are in the West. Because the story is little known in the West, Wizards of the Coast chose to distribute these cards primarily in Asia, with the English version slated for distribution mostly in Australia and New Zealand.

The *Portal Three Kingdoms* set includes one ability not found in other **Magic** sets: horsemanship. This is similar to flying. Creatures with horsemanship can be blocked only by other creatures with horsemanship.

Fitting a three-kingdom story into a five-color game required a bit of fiddling. The colors white, blue, and black represent the three kingdoms, and red and green were left as utility colors, designed to mix well with any of the other colors. This gives the set a different flavor.

Key Cards

Guan Yu, Sainted Warrior. Guan Yu is one of the main heroes of the Three Kingdoms story, so his card had to be good. It can almost never be permanently eliminated.

Sun Quan, Lord of Wu. The biggest of the blue Legends, Sun Quan turns all your creatures into cavalry. In a creature standoff this can mean immediate victory.

Cao Cao, Lord of Wei. Perhaps the strongest of the Legends, Cao Cao forces your opponent to play his or her spells immediately or lose them on your turn.

Sima Yi, Wei Field Marshal. If the game goes on long enough for you to get enough lands to play this Legend, it will usually be huge

enough to crush any creature your opponent can field.

The Story

The real events of this pivotal hundred-year stretch of Chinese history have fascinated people for centuries, inspiring countless artistic works and folk tales throughout Asia.

As the story begins, the Empire is beginning to splinter into three rival

kingdoms. To the north is Wei, led by the cunning and ruthless Cao Cao, who keeps the child emperor subservient to his own demands. Wu is to the south, led by the wise Sun Quan. To the west is Shu, ruled by the noble and virtuous Liu Bei, who becomes oath-brother to two of China's greatest heroes.

Countless soldiers fought during this turbulent period of dynastic change. The 1,000+ characters in the story illuminate the nature of power, the importance of diplomacy, and the intricacies of war.

Unless otherwise noted, all quotations on *Portal Three Kingdoms* cards are from the following work and are used with permission. Luo Guanzhong (attributed), *Three Kingdoms: A Historical Novel* (Beijing Foreign Language Press/Berkeley: University of California Press, 1991). Moss Roberts, trans.

ALERT SHU INFANTRY
Versions: 3K:U
Current Errata: **none**

AMBITION'S COST
Versions: 3K:R
Current Errata: **none**

BALANCE OF POWER
Versions: 3K:R
Current Errata: **none**

BARBARIAN GENERAL
Versions: 3K:U
Current Errata: **none**

BARBARIAN HORDE
Versions: 3K:C
Current Errata: **none**

BLAZE
Versions: 3K:U
Current Errata: **none**

BORROWING 100,000 ARROWS
Versions: 3K:U
Current Errata: **none**

BORROWING THE EAST WIND
Versions: 3K:R
Current Errata: **none**

BRILLIANT PLAN
Versions: 3K:U
Current Errata: **none**

BROKEN DAM
Versions: 3K:C
Current Errata: **none**

BURNING FIELDS
Versions: 3K:C
Current Errata: **none**

BURNING OF XINYE
Versions: 3K:R
Current Errata: **none**

CAO CAO, LORD OF WEI
Versions: 3K:R
Current Errata: **none**

CAO REN, WEI COMMANDER
Versions: 3K:R
Current Errata: **none**

CAPTURE OF JINGZHOU
Versions: 3K:R
Current Errata: **none**

CHAMPION'S VICTORY
Versions: 3K:U
Current Errata: **none**

COERCION
Versions: VI,TE,3K:C
Current Errata: **none**

CONTROL OF THE COURT
Versions: 3K:U
Current Errata: **none**

CORRUPT COURT OFFICIAL
Versions: 3K:U
Current Errata: **none**

CORRUPT EUNUCHS
Versions: 3K:U
Current Errata: **none**

COUNCIL OF ADVISORS
Versions: 3K:U
Current Errata: **none**

COUNTERINTELLIGENCE
Versions: 3K:U
Current Errata: **none**

CUNNING ADVISOR
Versions: 3K:U
Current Errata: **none**

DECEPTION
Versions: 3K:C
Current Errata: **none**

Desert Sandstorm 2🔴

Sorcery

Desert Sandstorm deals 1 damage to each creature. *(This includes your creatures.)*

While pursuing the remnants of Yuan Shao's forces into the Wuhan Desert, Cao Cao was temporarily turned back by a fierce sandstorm.

Illus. Xu Tan

DESERT SANDSTORM
Versions: 3K:C
Current Errata: **none**

Desperate Charge 2🔴

Sorcery

All your creatures get +2/+0 until the end of the turn.

"Lieutenants dishonored, corpses carted home; The general raises troops again to take revenge."

Illus. Chen Weidong

DESPERATE CHARGE
Versions: 3K:U
Current Errata: **none**

Diaochan, Artful Beauty 3🔴

Creature — Legend

On your turn, before you attack, you may tap Diaochan to destroy any one creature. Then, your opponent destroys any one creature of his or her choice.

Illus. Miao Aili 1/1

DIAOCHAN, ARTFUL BEAUTY
Versions: 3K:R
Current Errata: **none**

Dong Zhou, the Tyrant 4🔴

Creature — Legend

When Dong Zhou comes into play, choose one of your opponent's creatures. That creature deals damage to him or her equal to its power. *(Ignore this effect if your opponent doesn't have any creatures in play.)*

Illus. Junichi Inoue 3/3

DONG ZHOU, THE TYRANT
Versions: 3K:R
Current Errata: **none**

Eightfold Maze 2⚪

Sorcery

Play Eightfold Maze only after you're attacked, before you declare blockers.
Destroy any one attacking creature.

Illus. Shang Huitong
©1995–1999 Wizards of the Coast, Inc. 2/180

EIGHTFOLD MAZE
Versions: 3K:R
Current Errata: **none**

Empty City Ruse ⚪

Sorcery

Your opponent can't attack on his or her next turn.

Out of time and options, Kongming was forced to bluff at Xicheng. He tricked an army of 150,000 Wei by leaving the city gates open and calmly playing the zither.

Illus. Qu Xin
©1995–1999 Wizards of the Coast, Inc. 3/180

EMPTY CITY RUSE
Versions: 3K:U
Current Errata: **none**

Eunuchs' Intrigues 2🔴

Sorcery

Your opponent chooses one of his or her creatures. Only that creature can block this turn.

Taking control of powerful court positions one by one, eunuchs eventually brought on the fall of the Han dynasty, leading to the chaos of the three kingdoms.

Illus. Li Yousong

EUNUCHS' INTRIGUE
Versions: 3K:U
Current Errata: **none**

Exhaustion 2🔵

Sorcery

At the beginning of your opponent's next turn, he or she skips untapping creatures and lands.

Starving and worn, Cao Cao escaped from the battle of Red Cliffs with only 27 of his original 800,000 men.

Illus. Qu Xin
©1995–1999 Wizards of the Coast, Inc. 1/180

EXHAUSTION
Versions: US,3K:R
Current Errata: **none**

Extinguish 1🔵

Sorcery

Play Extinguish only in response to another player playing a sorcery. That sorcery has no effect, and that player puts it into his or her graveyard.

Illus. Ding Songjian
©1995–1999 Wizards of the Coast, Inc.

EXTINGUISH
Versions: 3K:R
Current Errata: **none**

False Defeat 3⚪

Sorcery

Take any one creature card from your graveyard and put that creature into play.

"All warfare is based on deception."
—Sun Tzu, Art of War (trans. Giles)

Illus. Li Wang
©1993–1999 Wizards of the Coast, Inc. 4/180

FALSE DEFEAT
Versions: 3K:C
Current Errata: **none**

False Mourning 🟢

Sorcery

Take any one card from your graveyard and put that card on the top of your library.

Zhou Yu, Sun Ce, and other famous generals feigned their deaths in order to later surprise their opponents.

Illus. Koji

FALSE MOURNING
Versions: 3K:U
Current Errata: **none**

Famine 3🔴🔴

Sorcery

Famine deals 3 damage to each creature and player. *(This includes your creatures and you.)*

"But it was a year of dearth. People were reduced to eating leaves of jujube trees. Corpses were seen everywhere in the countryside."

Illus. Sun Nan
©1993–1999 Wizards of the Coast, Inc. 75/180

FAMINE
Versions: 3K:U
Current Errata: **none**

FIRE AMBUSH
Versions: 3K:C
Current Errata: **none**

FIRE BOWMAN
Versions: 3K:U
Current Errata: **none**

FLANKING TROOPS
Versions: 3K:U
Current Errata: **none**

FORCED RETREAT
Versions: 3K:C
Current Errata: **none**

FOREST
Versions: 3K:L
Current Errata: **none**

FOREST
Versions: 3K:L
Current Errata: **none**

FOREST
Versions: 3K:L
Current Errata: **none**

FOREST BEAR
Versions: 3K:C
Current Errata: **none**

GHOSTLY VISIT
Versions: 3K:R
Current Errata: **none**

GUAN YU, SAINTED WARRIOR
Versions: 3K:R
Current Errata: **none**

GUAN YU'S 1,000-LI MARCH
Versions: 3K:R
Current Errata: **none**

HEAVY FOG
Versions: 3K:U
Current Errata: **none**

HUA TUO, HONORED PHYSICIAN
Versions: 3K:R
Current Errata: **none**

HUANG ZHONG, SHU GENERAL
Versions: 3K:R
Current Errata: **none**

HUNTING CHEETAH
Versions: 3K:U
Current Errata: **none**

IMPERIAL EDICT
Versions: 3K:C
Current Errata: **none**

IMPERIAL RECRUIT
Versions: 3K:U
Current Errata: **none**

IMPERIAL SEAL
Versions: 3K:R
Current Errata: **none**

INDEPENDENT TROOPS
Versions: 3K:C
Current Errata: **none**

ISLAND
Versions: 3K:L
Current Errata: **none**

ISLAND
Versions: 3K:L
Current Errata: **none**

ISLAND
Versions: 3K:L
Current Errata: **none**

KONGMING, "SLEEPING DRAGON"
Versions: 3K:R
Current Errata: **none**

KONGMING'S CONTRAPTIONS
Versions: 3K:R
Current Errata: **none**

LADY SUN
Versions: 3K:R
Current Errata: **none**

LADY ZHURONG, WARRIOR QUEEN
Versions: 3K:R
Current Errata: **none**

LIU BEI, LORD OF SHU
Versions: 3K:R
Current Errata: **none**

LONE WOLF
Versions: 3K:U
Current Errata: **none**

LOYAL RETAINERS
Versions: 3K:U
Current Errata: **none**

LU BU, MASTER-AT-ARMS
Versions: 3K:R
Current Errata: **none**

LU MENG, WU GENERAL
Versions: 3K:R
Current Errata: **none**

LU SU, WU ADVISOR
Versions: 3K:R
Current Errata: **none**

LU XUN, SCHOLAR GENERAL
Versions: 3K:R
Current Errata: **none**

MA CHAO, WESTERN WARRIOR
Versions: 3K:R
Current Errata: **none**

MARSHALING THE TROOPS
Versions: 3K:R
Current Errata: **none**

MENG HUO, BARBARIAN KING
Versions: 3K:R
Current Errata: **none**

MENG HUO'S HORDE
Versions: 3K:C
Current Errata: **none**

MISFORTUNE'S GAIN
Versions: 3K:C
Current Errata: **none**

MOUNTAIN
Versions: 3K:L
Current Errata: **none**

MOUNTAIN
Versions: 3K:L
Current Errata: **none**

MOUNTAIN
Versions: 3K:L
Current Errata: **none**

MOUNTAIN BANDIT
Versions: 3K:C
Current Errata: **none**

MYSTIC DENIAL
Versions: 3K:U
Current Errata: **none**

OVERWHELMING FORCES
Versions: 3K:R
Current Errata: **none**

PANG TONG, "YOUNG PHOENIX"
Versions: 3K:R
Current Errata: **none**

PEACH GARDEN OATH
Versions: 3K:U
Current Errata: **none**

PLAINS
Versions: 3K:L
Current Errata: **none**

PLAINS
Versions: 3K:L
Current Errata: **none**

PORTAL 3 KINGDOMS

PLAINS
Versions: 3K:L
Current Errata: **none**

POISON ARROW
Versions: 3K:U
Current Errata: **none**

PREEMPTIVE STRIKE
Versions: 3K:C
Current Errata: **none**

RALLY THE TROOPS
Versions: 3K:U
Current Errata: **none**

RAVAGES OF WAR
Versions: 3K:R
Current Errata: **none**

RAVAGING HORDE
Versions: 3K:U
Current Errata: **none**

RED CLIFFS ARMADA
Versions: 3K:U
Current Errata: **none**

RELENTLESS ASSAULT
Versions: VI,6E,3K:R
Current Errata: **none**

RENEGADE TROOPS
Versions: 3K:U
Current Errata: **none**

RETURN TO BATTLE
Versions: 3K:C
Current Errata: **none**

RIDING RED HARE
Versions: 3K:C
Current Errata: **none**

RIDING THE DILU HORSE
Versions: 3K:R
Current Errata: **none**

Rockslide Ambush

Sorcery

Rockslide Ambush deals to any one creature damage equal to the number of mountain cards you have in play. *(This includes both tapped and untapped mountain cards.)*

Illus. Inoue Junichi

ROCKSLIDE AMBUSH
Versions: 3K:U
Current Errata: **none**

Rolling Earthquake

Sorcery

Rolling Earthquake deals X damage to each player and each creature without horsemanship. *(This includes you and your creatures without horsemanship.)*

Illus. Yang Hong

ROLLING EARTHQUAKE
Versions: 3K:R
Current Errata: **none**

Sage's Knowledge

Sorcery

Return any one sorcery card from your graveyard to your hand.

"Those who know do not talk. Those who talk do not know."
—Lao Tzu, Tao Te Ching
(trans. Feng and English)

Illus. Ding Songjian

SAGE'S KNOWLEDGE
Versions: 3K:C
Current Errata: **none**

Shu Cavalry

Creature — Soldiers

Horsemanship

In establishing the Shu kingdom, Liu Bei's forces fought against Ma Chao at Chengdu. Eventually, Ma Chao surrendered and became one of Liu Bei's Tiger Generals.

Illus. Li Xiaohua

2/2

SHU CAVALRY
Versions: 3K:C
Current Errata: **none**

Shu Defender

Creature — Soldier

When Shu Defender blocks, it gets +0/+2 until the end of the turn.

Confronting Cao Cao's army at Steepslope Bridge, Zhang Fei bellowed, "I am Zhang Fei of Yan! Who dares fight me to the death?" Cao Cao's army cowered and fled.

Illus. Sun Nan

2/2

SHU DEFENDER
Versions: 3K:C
Current Errata: **none**

Shu Elite Companions

Creature — Soldiers

Horsemanship

Throughout the three kingdoms, important generals were often guarded by small groups of expert soldiers known as "elite companions."

Illus. Zhao Dafu

3/3

SHU ELITE COMPANIONS
Versions: 3K:U
Current Errata: **none**

Shu Elite Infantry

Creature — Soldiers

Kongming's first campaign against the Wei kingdom was a rousing success until an arrogant Shu general, Ma Su, foolishly lost the city of Jieting.

Illus. Song Shikai

3/3

SHU ELITE INFANTRY
Versions: 3K:C
Current Errata: **none**

Shu Farmer

Creature — Farmer

On your turn, before you attack, you may tap Shu Farmer to gain 1 life.

"The common folk are ceaselessly active. The fields are fertile and the soil productive, and neither flood nor drought plagues us."
—A Shu diplomat

Illus. Li Xiaohua

1/1

SHU FARMER
Versions: 3K:C
Current Errata: **none**

Shu Foot Soldiers

Creature — Soldiers

Liu Bei lost many men at the battle of Runan because of his lack of strategy. It wasn't until he met Kongming that he began to truly succeed as a leader.

Illus. Xu Tin

2/3

SHU FOOT SOLDIERS
Versions: 3K:C
Current Errata: **none**

Shu General

Creature — Soldier

Horsemanship
Attacking doesn't cause Shu General to tap.

Illus. Li Xiaohua

2/2

SHU GENERAL
Versions: 3K:U
Current Errata: **none**

Shu Grain Caravan

Creature — Soldiers

When Shu Grain Caravan comes into play, you gain 2 life.

Keeping a million-man army fed was no easy task. Grain and rice caravans were the lifeblood of the empire.

Illus. Li Wang

2/2

SHU GRAIN CARAVAN
Versions: 3K:C
Current Errata: **none**

Shu Soldier-Farmers

Creature — Soldiers

When Shu Soldier-Farmers comes into play, you gain 4 life.

During Kongming's campaigns against the Wei, his Shu troops rotated from the battlefront to the fields every hundred days.

Illus. Li Xiaohua

2/4

SHU SOLDIER-FARMERS
Versions: 3K:R
Current Errata: **none**

SIMA YI, WEI FIELD MARSHAL
Versions: 3K:R
Current Errata: **none**

SLASHING TIGER
Versions: 3K:R
Current Errata: **none**

SOUTHERN ELEPHANT
Versions: 3K:C
Current Errata: **none**

SPOILS OF VICTORY
Versions: 3K:U
Current Errata: **none**

SPRING OF ETERNAL PEACE
Versions: 3K:C
Current Errata: **none**

STALKING TIGER
Versions: 3K:C
Current Errata: **none**

STOLEN GRAIN
Versions: 3K:U
Current Errata: **none**

STONE CATAPULT
Versions: 3K:R
Current Errata: **none**

STONE RAIN
Versions: TE,IA,MI,RV,4E,5E,6E,PL,3K:C
Current Errata: **none**

STRATEGIC PLANNING
Versions: 3K:U
Current Errata: **none**

STRAW SOLDIERS
Versions: 3K:C
Current Errata: **none**

SUN CE, YOUNG CONQUEROR
Versions: 3K:R
Current Errata: **none**

SUN QUAN, LORD OF WU
Versions: **3K:R**
Current Errata: **none**

SWAMP
Versions: **3K:L**
Current Errata: **none**

SWAMP
Versions: **3K:L**
Current Errata: **none**

SWAMP
Versions: **3K:L**
Current Errata: **none**

TAOIST HERMIT
Versions: **3K:U**
Current Errata: **none**

TAOIST MYSTIC
Versions: **3K:R**
Current Errata: **none**

TAUNTING CHALLENGE
Versions: **3K:R**
Current Errata: **none**

THREE VISITS
Versions: **3K:C**
Current Errata: **none**

TRAINED CHEETAH
Versions: **3K:U**
Current Errata: **none**

TRAINED JACKAL
Versions: **3K:C**
Current Errata: **none**

TRIP WIRE
Versions: **3K:U**
Current Errata: **none**

VENGEANCE
Versions: **3K:U**
Current Errata: **none**

VIRTUOUS CHARGE
Versions: **3K:C**
Current Errata: **none**

VOLUNTEER MILITIA
Versions: **3K:C**
Current Errata: **none**

WARRIOR'S OATH
Versions: **3K:R**
Current Errata: **none**

WARRIOR'S STAND
Versions: **3K:U**
Current Errata: **none**

WEI AMBUSH FORCE
Versions: **3K:C**
Current Errata: **none**

WEI ASSASSINS
Versions: **3K:U**
Current Errata: **none**

WEI ELITE COMPANIONS
Versions: **3K:U**
Current Errata: **none**

WEI INFANTRY
Versions: **3K:C**
Current Errata: **none**

WEI NIGHT RAIDERS
Versions: **3K:U**
Current Errata: **none**

WEI SCOUT
Versions: **3K:C**
Current Errata: **none**

WEI STRIKE FORCE
Versions: **3K:C**
Current Errata: **none**

WEILDING THE GREEN DRAGON
Versions: **3K:C**
Current Errata: **none**

Wolf Pack — 6🌲🌲

Creature — Wolves

When Wolf Pack attacks and is blocked, you may have it deal its damage to the defending player instead of to the creatures blocking it.

Illus. Yang Jun Kwon

7/6

WOLF PACK
Versions: **3K:R**
Current Errata: **none**

Wu Admiral — 4🌐

Creature — Soldier

As long as your opponent has an island in play, Wu Admiral gets +1/+1.

The Wu kingdom's well-trained admirals were integral to the Southlands' victory at Red Cliffs as well as the kingdom's defense.

Illus. Zhang Jiazhen

3/3

WU ADMIRAL
Versions: **3K:U**
Current Errata: **none**

Wu Elite Cavalry — 3🌐

Creature — Soldiers

Horsemanship

At the second battle of Ruxu, the brave Wu general Gan Ning raided Cao Cao's camp of 400,000 men with only 100 cavalry. Not a single man or horse was lost.

Illus. Li Wang

2/3

WU ELITE CAVALRY
Versions: **3K:C**
Current Errata: **none**

Wu Infantry — 1🌐

Creature — Soldiers

The first battle of Hefei was Sun Quan's last as a field general. From then on he let his generals command in the field while he directed battle from behind the front lines.

Illus. Xu Xiaoming

2/1

WU INFANTRY
Versions: **3K:C**
Current Errata: **none**

Wu Longbowman — 2🌐

Creature — Soldier

On your turn, before you attack, you may tap Wu Longbowman to have it deal 1 damage to any one creature or player.

Illus. Xu Tan

1/1

WU LONGBOWMAN
Versions: **3K:U**
Current Errata: **none**

Wu Scout — 1🌐

Creature — Soldier

Horsemanship

When Wu Scout comes into play, look at your opponent's hand.

Illus. Jiaming

1/1

WU SCOUT
Versions: **3K:C**
Current Errata: **none**

Wu Spy — 1🌐

Creature — Soldier

When Wu Spy comes into play, look at the top two cards of any player's library. Put one of them back on the top of that player's library and the other in his or her graveyard.

Illus. Zhao Tan

1/1

WU SPY
Versions: **3K:U**
Current Errata: **none**

Wu Warship — 2🌐

Creature — Ship

Wu Warship can't attack unless the defending player has an island in play.

Both Wu and Wei warships patrolled the Yangtze River, the natural border between the two kingdoms.

Illus. Jiang Zhuqing

3/3

WU WARSHIP
Versions: **3K:C**
Current Errata: **none**

Xiahou Dun, the One-Eyed — 2🌑🌑

Creature — Legend

Horsemanship
On your turn, before you attack, you may put Xiahou Dun into your graveyard to return a black card from your graveyard to your hand.

Illus. Junko Taguchi

3/2

XIAHOU DUN, THE ONE-EYED
Versions: **3K:R**
Current Errata: **none**

Xun Yu, Wei Advisor — 1🌑🌑

Creature — Legend

On your turn, before you attack, you may tap Xun Yu to give one of your creatures +2/+0 until the end of the turn.

"A splendid talent, admired of all men! His folly lay in serving Cao Cao's power."

Illus. Jack Wei

1/1

XUN YU, WEI ADVISOR
Versions: **3K:R**
Current Errata: **none**

Yellow Scarves Cavalry — 1🔴

Creature — Soldiers

Horsemanship
Yellow Scarves Cavalry can't block.

Illus. Chen Weidong

1/1

YELLOW SCARVES CAVALRY
Versions: **3K:C**
Current Errata: **none**

Yellow Scarves General — 3🔴

Creature — Soldier

Horsemanship
Yellow Scarves General can't block.

Zhang Jue, leader of the Yellow Scarves rebellion, was a Taoist master and tutored his soldiers in those arts.

Illus. Chen Weidong

2/2

YELLOW SCARVES GENERAL
Versions: **3K:R**
Current Errata: **none**

YELLOW SCARVES TROOPS
Versions: 3K:C
Current Errata: **none**

YOUNG WEI RECRUITS
Versions: 3K:C
Current Errata: **none**

YUAN SHAO, THE INDECISIVE
Versions: 3K:R
Current Errata: **none**

YUAN SHAO'S INFANTRY
Versions: 3K:U
Current Errata: **none**

ZHANG FEI, FIERCE WARRIOR
Versions: 3K:R
Current Errata: **none**

ZHANG HE, WEI GENERAL
Versions: 3K:R
Current Errata: **none**

ZHANG LIAO, HERO OF HEFEI
Versions: 3K:R
Current Errata: **none**

ZHAO ZILONG, TIGER GENERAL
Versions: 3K:R
Current Errata: **none**

ZHOU YU, CHIEF COMMANDER
Versions: 3K:R
Current Errata: **none**

ZHUGE JIN, WU STRATEGIST
Versions: 3K:R
Current Errata: **none**

ZODIAC DOG
Versions: 3K:C
Current Errata: **none**

ZODIAC DRAGON
Versions: 3K:R
Current Errata: **none**

Zodiac Goat

Creature — Goat

Mountainwalk (If defending player has a mountain in play, Zodiac Goat can't be blocked.)

"... Near death in Baidi, having reigned three years, / Bei sadly placed his son in Kongming's care...."

Illus. Qi Baocheng

1/1

ZODIAC GOAT
Versions: **3K:C**
Current Errata: **none**

Zodiac Horse

Creature — Horse

Islandwalk (If defending player has an island in play, Zodiac Horse can't be blocked.)

"... First take Jingzhou, next the Riverlands; / On that rich region, base your own royal stand.'..."

Illus. Ai Desheng

3/3

ZODIAC HORSE
Versions: **3K:U**
Current Errata: **none**

Zodiac Monkey

Creature — Monkey

Forestwalk (If defending player has a forest in play, Zodiac Monkey can't be blocked.)

"... By six offensives from the hills of Qi / Kongming sought to change Han's destiny...."

Illus. Ai Desheng

2/1

ZODIAC MONKEY
Versions: **3K:C**
Current Errata: **none**

Zodiac Ox

Creature — Ox

Swampwalk (If defending player has a swamp in play, Zodiac Ox can't be blocked.)

"... Cao's abdication changed the face of all; / No mighty battles marked the Southland's fall...."

Illus. Ai Desheng

3/3

ZODIAC OX
Versions: **3K:U**
Current Errata: **none**

Zodiac Pig

Creature — Pig

Swampwalk (If defending player has a swamp in play, Zodiac Pig can't be blocked.)

"... Zhong Hui and Deng Ai next led armies west: / And to the Cao, Han's hills and streams now passed...."

Illus. Qi Baocheng

3/3

ZODIAC PIG
Versions: **3K:U**
Current Errata: **none**

Zodiac Rabbit

Creature — Rabbit

Forestwalk (If defending player has a forest in play, Zodiac Rabbit can't be blocked.)

"... The world's affairs rush on, an endless stream; / A sky-told fate, infinite in reach, dooms all...."

Illus. Ai Desheng

1/1

ZODIAC RABBIT
Versions: **3K:C**
Current Errata: **none**

Zodiac Rat

Creature — Rat

Swampwalk (If defending player has a swamp in play, Zodiac Rat can't be blocked.)

"... Cao Pi, Cao Rui, Fang, Mao, and briefly, Huan— / The Sima took the empire in their turn...."

Illus. Qi Baocheng

1/1

ZODIAC RAT
Versions: **3K:C**
Current Errata: **none**

Zodiac Rooster

Creature — Rooster

Plainswalk (If defending player has a plains in play, Zodiac Rooster can't be blocked.)

"... But the time of Han had run—could he [Kongming] not tell?— / That night his master star fell past the hills...."

Illus. Ai Desheng

2/1

ZODIAC ROOSTER
Versions: **3K:C**
Current Errata: **none**

Zodiac Snake

Creature — Snake

Swampwalk (If defending player has a swamp in play, Zodiac Snake can't be blocked.)

"Thrice Xuande's ardent quest led to Nanyang, / Where Sleeping Dragon unveiled Han's partition:..."

Illus. Qi Baocheng

2/2

ZODIAC SNAKE
Versions: **3K:C**
Current Errata: **none**

Zodiac Tiger

Creature — Tiger

Forestwalk. (If defending player has a forest in play, Zodiac Tiger can't be blocked.)

"... Three kings no more—Chenliu, Guiming, Anle. / The fiefs and posts must now be filled anew...."

Illus. Ai Desheng

3/4

ZODIAC TIGER
Versions: **3K:U**
Current Errata: **none**

Zuo Ci, the Mocking Sage

Creature — Legend

Zuo Ci can't be blocked by creatures with horsemanship.

Whenever your opponent chooses a creature in play, he or she can't choose Zuo Ci.

Illus. Wang Yuqun

1/1

ZUO CI, THE MOCKING SAGE
Versions: **3K:R**
Current Errata: **none**

UNGLUED UNGLUED UNGLUED UNGLUED UNGLUED UNGLUED UNGLUED UNGLUED
UNGLUED UNGLUED UNGLUED
™ ™
MAGIC
The Gathering ®
UNGLUED UNGLUED UNGLUED UNGLUED UNGLUED UNGLUED
UNGLUED UNGLUED UNGLUED

OVERVIEW

The *Unglued*™ supplement took off in a completely different direction from every other **Magic** set. Its goal was to put the "fun" back in the game for players who had been driven away by the strongly competitive environment fostered by big cash prize tournaments. *Unglued* cards weren't intended for serious or competitive play—indeed, they were banned from DCI tournaments even before publication, and they were marked with silver borders to make them easy to spot and remove when building serious decks. It was designed as more of a party game, with cards that required players to perform stunts, sing songs, speak in funny voices, and generally get as far away from being serious as possible. A few of the cards were created specifically to cause headaches for rules lawyers.

The *Unglued* creation also gave the designers a chance to poke fun at **Magic** history itself. Some of the cards are "in jokes" for longtime **Magic** players, with subtle or not-so-subtle references to famous cards and mistakes from older sets. Many of the cards bend the rules artistically as well as mechanically; the artwork creeps out of its normal boxed-in borders, jostling around the text and in one case even crossing over to another card.

As one more bit of wackiness, the set included a "secret message" from the designer. To see it, arrange the cards in numeric order and read the tiny word near the legal text on each one.

IMPORTANT CARDS

The *Unglued* supplement has few "power cards" to pick out, since it wasn't designed for power gamers. Instead, its best-known cards are famous for their jokes or for the stories behind them.

B.F.M. (Big Furry Monster): Definitely the most famous card(s) of the set, the 99/99 B.F.M. is *so* big that it can't fit on one card. Instead, it has a left-half card and a right-half card. You must use both cards together to play it. B.F.M. can also be brought into play by effects that move both cards simultaneously (like Living Death), but not by those that affect only one card (like Animate Dead).

Chaos Confetti: This card is based on a story from the early **Magic** days. The rare artifact Chaos Orb required its player to drop it onto the playing surface; Chaos Orb then destroyed everything it touched. According to **Magic** urban legend, someone won the final match of a big tournament by shredding his Chaos Orb and scattering the pieces over all his opponent's cards. Chaos Confetti uses this as an actual mechanic. The art on Chaos Confetti shows a Chaos Orb being torn.

Blacker Lotus and Cardboard Carapace: These cards parody the **Magic** player-collector's greed. Blacker Lotus is even more powerful than the original Black Lotus, but you have to rip the card up to use it…and it's rare. Cardboard Carapace gains power based on the number of additional copies of the card you have with you. (You don't actually have to own them, which leads to some amusing plays when a roomful of friends are playing *Unglued* games. "Can I borrow your Cardboard Carapaces for one turn?")

Incoming!: This spell takes the old Eureka spell to its limit, putting everything in the deck into play. All the players at the *Unglued* premiere received a giant version of this card.

Censorship: The art for this started life as the art for a regular **Magic** card. Part of it was cropped by the art director for being too suggestive. Of course, with all the black bars across it, identifying anything about Censorship's picture is a challenge!

Double Dip/Play/Deal/Take/Cross: These five cards (one for each color) each do something when they resolve and then do it again at the beginning of your next game with the same player. Their flavor text forms a limerick when read in the proper order.

Hurloon Wrangler: This minotaur's unique ability, "denimwalk," led to what has to be one of the most unusual rulings ever made by a **Magic** judge: removing your pants is faster than a mana source.

Volrath's Motion Sensor: Local enchantments are normally placed on top of whatever they enchant, so when the designers decided to create an "Enchant Player" card, it was obvious (by the distorted *Unglued* logic) that it should sit on the enchanted player. Combine Volrath's Motion Sensor with cards that require other actions (Ashnod's Coupon is a good one) for a real test of skill.

Infernal Spawn of Evil: "It's coming!" The art is the joke on this one—many **Magic** cards have been changed at the last moment when the picture that came back from the artist didn't match what the designers had intended.

Brass Calendar: Another art joke—the name and flavor text are a calendar, but the artwork is a colander. This hearkens back to an art mistake on one of the early **Magic** cards, Alchor's Tomb, which was supposed to be Alchor's Tome.

Look at Me, I'm the DCI: the exquisite artwork on this card (drawn by the set's designer, Mark Rosewater, who bought a whole new box of crayons just for this purpose) shows an insider's view of the methods used by the DCI when deciding which cards to restrict or ban.

Rock Lobster/Paper Tiger/ Scissors Lizard: Players sometimes refer to the **Magic** metagame as an elaborate version of rock-paper-scissors. These cards take it all the way.

Timmy, Power Gamer: Often mentioned in **Magic** design team meetings, this is the fellow those huge creatures are created for.

The Ultimate Nightmare of Wizards of the Coast® Customer Service: The Wizards of the Coast game support team is still threatening the designers with serious bodily harm over this one. True rules lawyers, however, complain that the card is far too simple. It's a red spell, not a blue spell, by the way—as any rules lawyer can tell you, the color of the mana (not the card's border) determines the color of the spell.

Tokens: The most-asked question at the *Unglued* premiere was "What are these cards with the big oval and no card type or casting cost?" These "token cards" don't count as cards for **Magic** rules purposes; they're just a prettier alternative to coins, candies, or whatever other small markers players had been using for cards that create token creatures.

Plains/Island/Swamp/Mountain/ Forest: The only serious cards in the *Unglued* set, these basic lands have no text box—the picture fills the entire card. These gorgeous lands became very popular with tournament players, who used them in regular decks. Each booster pack had one land, so in some circles they were traded like rares.

ASHNOD'S COUPON
Versions: **UG:R**
Current Errata: **none**

B.F.M. (BIG FURRY MONSTER LEFT)
Versions: **UG:R**
Current Errata: **none**

B.F.M. (BIG FURRY MONSTER RIGHT)
Versions: **UG:R**
Current Errata: **none**

BLACKER LOTUS
Versions: **UG:R**
Current Errata: **none**

BRONZE CALENDAR
Versions: **UG:U**
Current Errata: **none**

BUREAUCRACY
Versions: **UG:R**
Current Errata: **none**

BRUNING CINDER FURY OF CRIMSON CHAOS FIRE
Versions: **UG:R**
Current Errata: **none**

CARDBOARD CARAPACE
Versions: **UG:R**
Current Errata: **none**

CENSORSHIP
Versions: **UG:U**
Current Errata: **none**

CHAOS CONFETTI
Versions: **UG:C**
Current Errata: **none**

CHARM SCHOOL
Versions: **UG:U**
Current Errata: **none**

CHECKS AND BALANCES
Versions: **UG:U**
Current Errata: **none**

CHICKEN A LA KING
Versions: UG:R
Current Errata: **none**

CHICKEN EGG
Versions: UG:C
Current Errata: **none**

CLAM SESSION
Versions: UG:C
Current Errata: **none**

CLAM-I-AM
Versions: UG:C
Current Errata: **none**

CLAMBASSADORS
Versions: UG:C
Current Errata: **none**

CLAY PIGEON
Versions: UG:U
Current Errata: **none**

COMMON COURTESY
Versions: UG:U
Current Errata: **none**

DEADHEAD
Versions: UG:C
Current Errata: **none**

DENIED!
Versions: UG:C
Current Errata: **none**

DOUBLE CROSS
Versions: UG:C
Current Errata: **none**

DOUBLE DEAL
Versions: UG:C
Current Errata: **none**

DOUBLE DIP
Versions: UG:C
Current Errata: **none**

DOUBLE PLAY
Versions: UG:C
Current Errata: **none**

DOUBLE TAKE
Versions: UG:C
Current Errata: **none**

ELVISH IMPERSONATORS
Versions: UG:C
Current Errata: **none**

FLOCK OF RABID SHEEP
Versions: UG:U
Current Errata: **none**

FOREST
Versions: UG:L
Current Errata: **none**

FOWL PLAY
Versions: UG:C
Current Errata: **none**

FREE-FOR-ALL
Versions: UG:R
Current Errata: **none**

FREE-RANGE CHICKEN
Versions: UG:C
Current Errata: **none**

GERRYMANDERING
Versions: UG:U
Current Errata: **none**

GET A LIFE
Versions: UG:U
Current Errata: **none**

GHAZBÁN OGRESS
Versions: UG:C
Current Errata: **none**

GIANT FAN
Versions: UG:R
Current Errata: **none**

GOBLIN BOOKIE
Versions: UG:C
Current Errata: **none**

GOBLIN BOWLING TEAM
Versions: UG:C
Current Errata: **none**

GOBLIN (TOKEN)
Versions: UG:C
Current Errata: **none**

GOBLIN TUTOR
Versions: UG:U
Current Errata: **none**

GROWTH SPURT
Versions: UG:C
Current Errata: **none**

GUS
Versions: UG:C
Current Errata: **none**

HANDCUFFS
Versions: UG:U
Current Errata: **none**

HUNGRY HUNGRY HEIFER
Versions: UG:U
Current Errata: **none**

HURLOON WRANGLER
Versions: UG:C
Current Errata: **none**

I'M RUBBER, YOU'RE GLUE
Versions: UG:R
Current Errata: **none**

INCOMING!
Versions: UG:R
Current Errata: **none**

INFERNAL SPAWN OF EVIL
Versions: UG:R
Current Errata: **none**

ISLAND
Versions: UG:L
Current Errata: **none**

JACK-IN-THE-MOX
Versions: UG:R
Current Errata: **none**

JALUM GRIFTER
Versions: UG:R
Current Errata: **none**

JESTER'S SOMBRERO
Versions: UG:R
Current Errata: **none**

JUMBO IMP
Versions: UG:U
Current Errata: **none**

KNIGHT OF THE HOKEY POKEY
Versions: UG:C
Current Errata: **none**

KRAZY KOW
Versions: UG:C
Current Errata: **none**

LANDFILL
Versions: UG:R
Current Errata: **none**

LEXIVORE
Versions: UG:U
Current Errata: **none**

LOOK AT ME, I'M THE DCI
Versions: UG:R
Current Errata: **none**

MESA CHICKEN
Versions: UG:C
Current Errata: **none**

MINE, MINE, MINE!
Versions: UG:R
Current Errata: **none**

MIRROR MIRROR
Versions: **UG:R**
Current Errata: **none**

MISS DEMEANOR
Versions: **UG:U**
Current Errata: **none**

MOUNTAIN
Versions: **UG:L**
Current Errata: **none**

ONCE MORE WITH FEELING
Versions: **UG:R**
Current Errata: **none**

ORGAN HARVEST
Versions: **UG:C**
Current Errata: **none**

OW
Versions: **UG:R**
Current Errata: **none**

PAPER TIGER
Versions: **UG:C**
Current Errata: **none**

PEGASUS (TOKEN)
Versions: **UG:U**
Current Errata: **none**

PLAINS
Versions: **UG:L**
Current Errata: **none**

POULTRYGEIST
Versions: **UG:C**
Current Errata: **none**

PRISMATIC WARDROBE
Versions: **UG:C**
Current Errata: **none**

PSYCHIC NETWORK
Versions: **UG:R**
Current Errata: **none**

RICOCHET
Versions: **UG:U**
Current Errata: **none**

ROCK LOBSTER
Versions: **UG:C**
Current Errata: **none**

SCISSORS LIZARD
Versions: **UG:C**
Current Errata: **none**

SEX APPEAL
Versions: **UG:C**
Current Errata: **none**

SHEEP (TOKEN)
Versions: **UG:U**
Current Errata: **none**

SOLDIER (TOKEN)
Versions: **UG:U**
Current Errata: **none**

SORRY
Versions: **UG:U**
Current Errata: **none**

SPARK FIEND
Versions: **UG:R**
Current Errata: **none**

SPATULA OF THE AGES
Versions: **UG:U**
Current Errata: **none**

SQUIRREL (TOKEN)
Versions: **UG:U**
Current Errata: **none**

SQUIRREL FARM
Versions: **UG:R**
Current Errata: **none**

STRATEGY, SCHMATEGY
Versions: **UG:R**
Current Errata: **none**

SWAMP
Versions: UG:L
Current Errata: **none**

TEAM SPIRIT
Versions: UG:C
Current Errata: **none**

TEMP OF THE DAMNED
Versions: UG:C
Current Errata: **none**

THE CHEESE STANDS ALONE
Versions: UG:R
Current Errata: **none**

THE ULTIMATE NIGHTMARE OF WIZARDS OF THE COAST(R) CUSTOMER SERVICE
Versions: UG:U
Current Errata: **none**

TIMMY, POWER GAMER
Versions: UG:R
Current Errata: **none**

URZA'S CONTACT LENSES
Versions: UG:U
Current Errata: **none**

URZA'S SCIENCE FAIR PROJECT
Versions: UG:U
Current Errata: **none**

VOLRATH'S MOTION SENSOR
Versions: UG:U
Current Errata: **none**

ZOMBIE (TOKEN)
Versions: UG:U
Current Errata: **none**

STARTER™

The *Magic: The Gathering—Starter* set is the latest attempt by Wizards of the Coast to ease new players into the game. It simply leaves out elements unnecessary for basic game play, such as artifacts, instant spells, and complicated abilities.

The *Starter* set is only slightly larger than a standard **Magic** expansion. Most of its cards are reprints of cards already available, with their text boxes modified to make the distinction between rules text and flavor text

clearer. The *Starter* set does contain twenty-six new cards created just for this release. Like *Classic* (Sixth Edition) cards, *Starter* cards are available in a fixed-deck game, randomized boosters, and preconstructed decks (one for each color).

The *Starter* game comes with two decks, two playmats, a step-by-step play guide, and a simplified version of the **Magic: The Gathering** rulebook. This game contains eight cards not available in boosters, four of which haven't been printed anywhere else (see "Key Cards" below), so anyone wishing to acquire a complete set of *Starter* cards will need to purchase a game box.

KEY CARDS

Here are a few of the more interesting cards created for the *Starter* set.

Eager Cadet, Royal Falcon, Sea Eagle, and Willow Elf: These four cards are found only in the *Starter* game. This is their only claim to fame; they have no special abilities and aren't any better than other easily available creatures, so only "completist" collectors need be concerned about them.

Champion Lancer. Six mana for a 3/3 creature is a lot, but in a creature-heavy environment, this Knight is nearly invincible.

Silverback Ape. The opposite end of the spectrum from the Champion Lancer, the Ape has no abilities at all, but it does have the best ratio in the game of power/toughness to cost.

Vizzerdrix. This big blue creature is cousin to the *Tempest* black creature Kezzerdrix. Vizzerdrix starred in one of the **Magic: The Gathering** TV commercials that aired in the U.S. during 1999.

Trained Orgg. The other **Magic** TV star, this beastie got to beat up Bob from Accounting in a 1999 TV commercial. Trained Orgg costs two more mana than the original Orgg from the *Fallen Empires*™ and *Fifth Edition* sets, but this one doesn't suffer from the restrictions on attacking and blocking that plagued its wilder relation.

Grim Tutor. This is an improved version of Vampiric Tutor from the basic set. Grim Tutor costs two more mana but gives you the card immediately rather than just putting it on top of your library.

Goblin Settler. Many standard **Magic** players would like this Goblin for their own decks. For one more mana than Stone Rain—which simply destroys a land—you get to both destroy a land and add a 1/1 Goblin to your army.

ABYSSAL HORROR
Versions: US,6E,6S:R
Current Errata: none

AIR ELEMENTAL
Versions: A,B,UL,RV,4E,5E,SA,6S:U
Current Errata: none

ALLURING SCENT
Versions: PL,SA,6S:R
Current Errata: none

ANCIENT CRAVING
Versions: SA,6E:R
Current Errata: none

ANGEL OF LIGHT
Versions: 6S:U
Current Errata: none

ANGEL OF MERCY
Versions: SA,6S:U
Current Errata: none

ANGELIC BLESSING
Versions: EX,SA,PL,6E:C
Current Errata: none

ARCHANGEL
Versions: VI,SA,PL,6E,6S:R
Current Errata: none

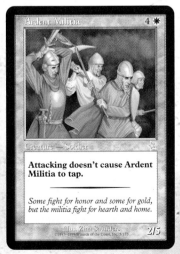

ARDENT MILITIA
Versions: WE,PL,6E,6S:U
Current Errata: none

ARMAGEDDON
Versions: A,B,UL,RV,4E,5E,6E,PL,SA,6S:R
Current Errata: none

BARBTOOTH WURM
Versions: SA,6S:C
Current Errata: none

BARGAIN
Versions: SA,6E:U
Current Errata: none

BLINDING LIGHT
Versions: MI:U,PL,6S:R
Current Errata: none

BOG IMP
Versions: DK,RV,4E,5E,6E,PL,6S:C
Current Errata: none

BOG RAIDERS
Versions: SA,US,6S:C
Current Errata: none

BOG WRAITH
Versions: A,B,UL,RV,4E,5E,6E,PL, 6S:U
Current Errata: none

BORDER GUARD
Versions: PL,6S:C
Current Errata: none

BREATH OF LIFE
Versions: PL,SA,6S:C
Current Errata: none

BULL HIPPO
Versions: US,PL,6S:U
Current Errata: none

CHAMPION LANCER
Versions: 6S:R
Current Errata: none

CHARGING PALADIN
Versions: PL,EX,6S:C
Current Errata: none

CHORUS OF WOE
Versions: SA,6S:C
Current Errata: none

CINDER STORM
Versions: 6S:U
Current Errata: none

COERCION
Versions: VI,TE: C 6E,3K,SA,6S:U
Current Errata: none

CORAL EEL
Versions: PL,6S:C
Current Errata: none

COUNTERSPELL
Versions: TE,IA,A,B,UL,RV,4E,5E,6E,6S:C
Current Errata: none

DAKMOR GHOUL
Versions: 6S:U
Current Errata: none

DAKMOR LANCER
Versions: 6S:R
Current Errata: none

DAKMOR PLAGUE
Versions: SA,6S:U
Current Errata: none

DAKMOR SCORPION
Versions: SA,6S:C
Current Errata: none

DAKMOR SORCERESS
Versions: SA,6S:R
Current Errata: none

DARK OFFERING
Versions: SA,6S:U
Current Errata: none

DENIZEN OF THE DEEP
Versions: SA,6S:R
Current Errata: none

DEVASTATION
Versions: PL,6S:R
Current Errata: none

DEVOTED HERO
Versions: PL,6S:C
Current Errata: none

DEVOUT MONK
Versions: 6S:C
Current Errata: none

DREAD REAPER
Versions: PL,6S:R
Current Errata: **none**

DURKWOOD BOARS
Versions: LG,4E,5E,6S:C
Current Errata: **none**

EAGER CADET
Versions: 6S:R
Current Errata: **none**

EARTH ELEMENTAL
Versions: A,B,UL,RV,4E,6S:U
Current Errata: **none**

EXHAUSTION
Versions: US:U PL,SA,6S:R
Current Errata: **none**

EXTINGUISH
Versions: 3K,SA,6S:C
Current Errata: **none**

EYE SPY
Versions: SA,6S:U
Current Errata: **none**

FALSE PEACE
Versions: PL,6S:C
Current Errata: **none**

FERAL SHADOW
Versions: MI,PL,6E,6S:C
Current Errata: **none**

FIRE ELEMENTAL
Versions: A,B,UL,RV,4E,6E,6S:U
Current Errata: **none**

FIRE TEMPEST
Versions: PL,6S:R
Current Errata: **none**

FOOT SOLDIERS
Versions: PL,6E:C
Current Errata: **none**

FOREST
Versions: 6S:L
Current Errata: **none**

FOREST
Versions: 6S:L
Current Errata: **none**

FOREST
Versions: 6S:L
Current Errata: **none**

FOREST
Versions: 6S:L
Current Errata: **none**

GERRARD'S WISDOM
Versions: WE,6S:U
Current Errata: **none**

GIANT OCTOPUS
Versions: PL,6E:C
Current Errata: **none**

GOBLIN CAVALIERS
Versions: SA,6S:C
Current Errata: **none**

GOBLIN CHARIOT
Versions: 6S:C
Current Errata: **none**

GOBLIN COMMANDO
Versions: 6S:U
Current Errata: **none**

GOBLIN GENERAL
Versions: SA,6S:R
Current Errata: **none**

GOBLIN GLIDER
Versions: SA,6S:C
Current Errata: **none**

GOBLIN HERO
Versions: DK,5E,6E,6S:R
Current Errata: **none**

GOBLIN LORE
Versions: SA,6S:U
Current Errata: **none**

GOBLIN MOUNTAINEER
Versions: SA,6S: C
Current Errata: **none**

GOBLIN SETTLER
Versions: 6S:U
Current Errata: **none**

GORILLA WARRIOR
Versions: PL,6S:C
Current Errata: **none**

GRAVEDIGGER
Versions: TE,PL,6E,6S:C
Current Errata: **none**

GRIM TUTOR
Versions: 6S:R
Current Errata: **none**

GRIZZLY BEARS
Versions: PL,A,B,UL,RV,4E,5E,6E,6S:C
Current Errata: **none**

HAND OF DEATH
Versions: PL,SA,6S:C
Current Errata: **none**

HOLLOW DOGS
Versions: 6S:C
Current Errata: **none**

HOWLING FURY
Versions: PL,6S:C
Current Errata: **none**

HULKING GOBLIN
Versions: 6S:C
Current Errata: **none**

HULKING OGRE
Versions: PL,6S:C
Current Errata: **none**

INGENIOUS THIEF
Versions: PL,6S:U
Current Errata: none

ISLAND
Versions: 6S:L
Current Errata: none

ISLAND
Versions: 6S:L
Current Errata: none

ISLAND
Versions: 6S:L
Current Errata: none

ISLAND
Versions: 6S:L
Current Errata: none

JAGGED LIGHTNING
Versions: US,SA,6S:U
Current Errata: none

KNIGHT ERRANT
Versions: PL,6S:C
Current Errata: none

LAST CHANCE
Versions: PL,6S:R
Current Errata: none

LAVA AXE
Versions: UL,PL,SA,6S:C
Current Errata: none

LONE WOLF
Versions: UL,SA,3K:U
Current Errata: none

LOYAL SENTRY
Versions: 6S:R
Current Errata: none

LYNX
Versions: SA,6S:C
Current Errata: none

137

MAN-O'-WAR
Versions: VI:C,PL,6S:U
Current Errata: **none**

MERFOLK OF THE PEARL TRIDENT
Versions: A,B,UL,RV,4E,5E,6E,PL,6S:C
Current Errata: **none**

MIND ROT
Versions: PL,SA:C
Current Errata: **none**

MONS'S GOBLIN RAIDERS
Versions: A,B,UL,RV,4E,5E:C 6S: R
Current Errata: **none**

MONSTROUS GROWTH
Versions: PL,SA:C
Current Errata: **none**

MOON SPRITE
Versions: PL,6S:U
Current Errata: **none**

MOUNTAIN
Versions: 6S:L
Current Errata: **none**

MOUNTAIN
Versions: 6S:L
Current Errata: **none**

MOUNTAIN
Versions: 6S:L
Current Errata: **none**

MOUNTAIN
Versions: 6S:L
Current Errata: **none**

MUCK RATS
Versions: PL,SA,6S:C
Current Errata: **none**

NATURAL SPRING
Versions: TE:C PL,SA,6S:U
Current Errata: **none**

NATURE'S CLOAK
Versions: PL,6S:R
Current Errata: **none**

NATURE'S LORE
Versions: IA: U 5E,PL,6S:C
Current Errata: **none**

NORWOOD ARCHERS
Versions: SA,6S:C
Current Errata: **none**

NORWOOD RANGERS
Versions: SA,6S:C
Current Errata: **none**

OGRE WARRIOR
Versions: SA,6S:C
Current Errata: **none**

OWL FAMILIAR
Versions: PL,6S:C
Current Errata: **none**

PATH OF PEACE
Versions: US,PL,SA,6S:C
Current Errata: **none**

PHANTOM WARRIOR
Versions: WE,6:U 6S:R
Current Errata: **none**

PIRACY
Versions: SA,6S
Current Errata: **none**

PLAINS
Versions: 6S:L
Current Errata: **none**

PLAINS
Versions: 6S:L
Current Errata: **none**

PLAINS
Versions: 6S:L
Current Errata: **none**

PLAINS
Versions: 6S:L
Current Errata: **none**

You may have Pride of Lions deal its combat damage to defending player as though it weren't blocked.

4/4

PRIDE OF LIONS
Versions: 6S:U
Current Errata: **none**

If the difference between your life total and target player's life total is 5 or less, exchange life totals with that player.

PSYCHIC TRANSFER
Versions: MI,6E,6S:R
Current Errata: **none**

Haste (This creature may attack the turn it comes into play.)

He raged at the world, at his family, at his life. But mostly he just raged.

1/1

RAGING GOBLIN
Versions: EX,PL,SA,6E,6S:C
Current Errata: **none**

Return target creature card from your graveyard to your hand.

The earth cannot hold that which magic commands.

RAISE DEAD
Versions: A,B,UL,RV,4E,5E,6E,PL,SA,6S:C
Current Errata: **none**

Look at the top five cards of target player's library. Put any number of them on the bottom of that library in any order and the rest on top of the library in any order.

RANSACK
Versions: ST,6S:U
Current Errata: **none**

When Ravenous Rats comes into play, target player chooses and discards a card from his or her hand.

1/1

RAVENOUS RATS
Versions: SA,6S:C
Current Errata: **none**

Return target instant or sorcery card from your graveyard to your hand.

The hardest lessons to grasp are the ones you've already learned.

RELEARN
Versions: WE,6E,6S:U
Current Errata: **none**

Untap all creatures that attacked this turn. You get another combat phase, followed by another main phase, this turn.

RELENTLESS ASSAULT
Versions: SA,3K,VI,6E,6S:R
Current Errata: **none**

Counter target creature spell.

When your enemies are denied soldiers, they are denied victory.

REMOVE SOUL
Versions: LG,CH,5E,6E,6S:C
Current Errata: **none**

Shuffle any number of creature cards from your graveyard into your library.

Death just encourages life the more.

RENEWING TOUCH
Versions: SA,6S:U
Current Errata: **none**

Creatures you control get +2/+2 until end of turn.

Bravery shines brightest in a pure soul.

RIGHTEOUS CHARGE
Versions: SA,6S:C
Current Errata: **none**

RIGHTEOUS FURY
Versions: SA,6S:R
Current Errata: **none**

ROYAL FALCON
Versions: 6S:C
Current Errata: **none**

ROYAL TROOPER
Versions: 6S:U
Current Errata: **none**

SACRED NECTAR
Versions: PL,6S:C
Current Errata: **none**

SCATHE ZOMBIES
Versions: A,B,UL,RV,4E,5E,6E,6S:C
Current Errata: **none**

SCORCHING SPEAR
Versions: PL,6S:C
Current Errata: **none**

SEA EAGLE
Versions: 6S:C
Current Errata: **none**

SERPENT WARRIOR
Versions: ST,PL,6S:C
Current Errata: **none**

SHRIEKING SPECTER
Versions: 6S:U
Current Errata: **none**

SILVERBACK APE
Versions: 6S:U
Current Errata: **none**

SLEIGHT OF HAND
Versions: SA,6S:C
Current Errata: **none**

SNAPPING DRAKE
Versions: PL,6S:C
Current Errata: **none**

SOUL FEAST
Versions: 6S:U
Current Errata: **none**

SOUTHERN ELEPHANT
Versions: 3K,6S:C
Current Errata: **none**

SPITTING EARTH
Versions: MI,PL,SA,6E,6S:C
Current Errata: **none**

SQUALL
Versions: 6S:C
Current Errata: **none**

STEADFASTNESS
Versions: PL,6S:C
Current Errata: **none**

STONE RAIN
Versions: TE,IA,MI,RV,4E,5E,6E,PL,SA,
3K,6S:C
Current Errata: **none**

STORM CROW
Versions: AL,PL,6E,6S:C
Current Errata: **none**

STREAM OF ACID
Versions: 6S:U
Current Errata: **none**

SUMMER BLOOM
Versions: VI: U PL,6E,6S:R
Current Errata: **none**

SWAMP
Versions: 6S:L
Current Errata: **none**

SWAMP
Versions: 6S:L
Current Errata: **none**

SWAMP
Versions: 6S:L
Current Errata: **none**

SWAMP
Versions: 6S:L
Current Errata: none

SYLVAN BASILISK
Versions: SA,6S:R
Current Errata: none

SYLVAN YETI
Versions: SA,6S:R
Current Errata: none

THORN ELEMENTAL
Versions: 6S:R
Current Errata: none

THUNDER DRAGON
Versions: 6S:R
Current Errata: none

TIDINGS
Versions: 6S:U
Current Errata: none

TIME EBB
Versions: TE,PL,SA,6S:C
Current Errata: none

TIME WARP
Versions:TE,6S:R
Current Errata: none

TOUCH OF BRILLIANCE
Versions: PL,SA,6S:C
Current Errata: none

TRAINED ORGG
Versions: 6S:R
Current Errata: none

TREMOR
Versions: VI,SA,6E,6S:C
Current Errata: none

UNDO
Versions:VI:C SA,6S:U
Current Errata: none

UNTAMED WILDS
Versions: LG,4E,5E,PL,SA,6E,6S:U
Current Errata: none

VENERABLE MONK
Versions: ST,PL,6E,6S:U
Current Errata: none

VENGEANCE
Versions: PL,SA,6S:U
Current Errata: none

VETERAN CAVALIER
Versions: 6S:U
Current Errata: none

VIZZERDRIX
Versions: 6S:R
Current Errata: none

VOLCANIC DRAGON
Versions: MI,PL,6E,6S:R
Current Errata: none

VOLCANIC HAMMER
Versions: PL,6S:C
Current Errata: none

WATER ELEMENTAL
Versions: A,B,UL,RV,4E,6S:U
Current Errata: none

WHIPTAIL WURM
Versions: PL,6S:U
Current Errata: none

WHIRLWIND
Versions: US,6S:R
Current Errata: none

WICKED PACT
Versions: PL,6S:R
Current Errata: none

WILD GRIFFIN
Versions: SA,6S:C
Current Errata: none

WILD OX
Versions: **SA,6S:U**
Current Errata: **none**

WILLOW ELF
Versions: **6S:C**
Current Errata: **none**

WIND DRAKE
Versions: **TE,PL,6S:C**
Current Errata: **none**

WIND SAIL
Versions: **SA,6S:C**
Current Errata: **none**

WOOD ELVES
Versions: **EX:C PL,6S:R**
Current Errata: **none**

1998 World Championship Decks

The 1998 World Championships took place in August in Seattle, Washington. The five-day event gathered a total of 203 players from 37 countries. The first three days were filled by 21 rounds of individual competition using Swiss pairings, with a different format for each day: Booster Draft, Standard Constructed deck, and Rath Cycle™ Constructed deck. The fourth day was for team competition; individual players who weren't members of national teams had the day free (though most used it for challenge matches or side tournaments). On the fifth and final day, the eight players with the top individual scores battled for the Champion title.

The 1998 World Championship decks duplicate four of the top Standard decks from the tournament. This is the third set of commemorative decks Wizards has published. Cards in the 1998 Championship decks, like the previous commerative decks, have gold borders and gold-printed signatures on their faces, indicating which player's deck each card came from. The signatures are helpful when you've mixed cards and want to put the original deck back together. The deck backs are black with a Pro Tour logo, so you can't mix these in a deck with regular **Magic** cards unless you're using opaque card sleeves. They're not legal for DCI tournament play even with sleeves.

The first two commemorative sets (from the first Pro Tour and the 1997 World Championships, respectively) featured the top decks from the tournament finals. For the 1998 decks, this wouldn't have given much variety. Four of the eight finalists played variants of a single deck, known as "Nightmare Survival." Three more played Sligh decks. To give a more interesting selection, Wizards chose the top deck in each of those two groups along with the remaining deck from the finals, Brian Hacker's white weenie deck. For the fourth deck they went 12th place for Randy Buehler's permission deck.

BRIAN SELDEN— 1998 World Champion

Brian Selden's decklist	2 Scroll Rack
4 Birds of Paradise	3 City of Brass
1 Cloudchaser Eagle	8 Forest
1 Man-o'-War	1 Gemstone Mine
2 Nekrataal	2 Karplusan Forest
1 Orcish Settlers	2 Reflecting Pool
2 Spike Feeder	1 Swamp
1 Spike Weaver	2 Underground River
1 Spirit of the Night	2 Undiscovered Paradise
1 Thrull Surgeon	1 Volrath's Stronghold
1 Tradewind Rider	
2 Uktabi Orangutan	**Sideboard**
1 Verdant Force	4 Boil
4 Wall of Blossoms	2 Dread of Night
2 Wall of Roots	3 Emerald Charm
2 Firestorm	1 Hall of Gemstone
1 Lobotomy	2 Phyrexian Furnace
4 Recurring Nightmare	2 Pyroblast
4 Survival of the Fittest	1 Staunch Defenders

Brian Selden played a version of the Nightmare Survival deck called "Cali Nightmare." Various versions of this deck were extremely popular in California for the month prior to Worlds; the strong competition there forced the deck to evolve quickly.

Nightmare Survival had its roots in a Living Death deck designed by Darwin Kastle. A lot of the players at the tournament referred to this entire class of decks as Living Death decks, even though some versions (including Selden's) had evolved far enough from

their roots to completely eliminate the Living Death.

The basic strategy of Selden's deck is to use Wall of Blossoms, Wall of Roots, and Spike Feeders to defend against early attacks until its player can draw Survival of the Fittest. Once Survival of the Fittest is in play, the player can discard creatures at will to fetch any of the various creatures with useful comes-into-play effects. The Survival player can retrieve whatever's needed to deal with the current game situation: Nekrataal to destroy creatures, Uktabi Orangutan to destroy artifacts, Cloudchaser Eagle to destroy enchantments…and, of course, more Walls of Blossoms for additional cards and Spike Feeders if running low on life.

The second half of the combo is Recurring Nightmare. This enchantment allows the deck to reuse the comes-into-play effects over and over again, cycling the creatures back and forth from its graveyard to play and producing their effect each time. This is why most of the creatures in the deck have only one copy rather than the three or four typical for most deck types.

The deck also contains two big monsters, Spirit of the Night and Verdant Force. Once one of those has been discarded and popped back into play by Recurring Nightmare, the game is virtually over.

The deck's main weakness is land destruction. Because the deck uses all five colors, it relies largely on nonbasic lands for its mana production. A Lobotomy that catches Survival of the Fittest or Recurring Nightmare will also severely cripple the deck.

BEN RUBIN—
Finalist, 1998 Worlds

Ben Rubin played what's commonly called a "Sligh" deck—that is, a fast mono-red deck featuring very cost-effective small creatures along with plenty of direct damage. This style of deck was first popularized for tournament play by Paul Sligh, who went nearly undefeated in a Pro Qualifier tournament back in April 1996 using a deck designed by Jay

Schneider. He raised eyebrows by using cards previously considered "junk creatures," such as Ironclaw Orcs. The deck quickly became a favorite and has remained one of the top tournament deck archetypes through all the format changes and set rotations since that time.

Rubin credited David Price (of Team Deadguy, designer of the "Deadguy Red" version of the Sligh deck) with convincing him that fast mono-red was the best choice for the 1998 World Championship environment. However, Rubin designed his own version rather than copying one from the Net. "Instead of using Fireslinger, which is the traditional two–casting-cost creature along with Ironclaw Orcs, I used Mogg Flunkies because of its power and [because] it's more aggressive than Fireslinger," Rubin said. In addition to the Flunkies, Rubin included two other creatures not found in the other top decks of this category: Goblin Vandal and Viashino Sandstalker.

Rubin's sideboard was very different from the sideboard used by John Finkel and Chris Pikula, the

other finalists playing decks of this type. All three were better prepared for blue opponents than for the green-black graveyard recursion decks they ended up facing in the finals. However, Rubin's Dwarven Miners (to destroy nonbasic lands) and Dwarven Thaumaturgists (to destroy 0-power Walls, especially Wall of Blossoms) proved extremely potent against these opponents. Finkel and Pikula's version had Phyrexian Furnaces to use against the graveyard-based decks, but these turned out to be less useful—both because Survival of the Fittest could dump so many cards into the graveyard so quickly, and because Uktabi Orangutan can easily get rid of the Furnace.

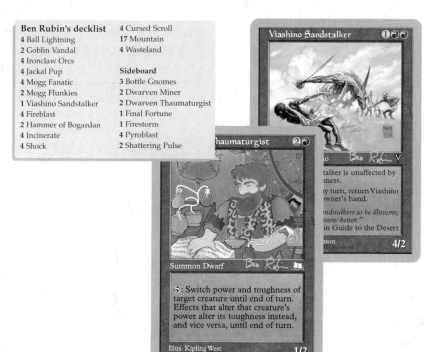

Ben Rubin's decklist

4 Ball Lightning	4 Cursed Scroll
2 Goblin Vandal	17 Mountain
4 Ironclaw Orcs	4 Wasteland
4 Jackal Pup	
4 Mogg Fanatic	**Sideboard**
2 Mogg Flunkies	3 Bottle Gnomes
1 Viashino Sandstalker	2 Dwarven Miner
4 Fireblast	2 Dwarven Thaumaturgist
2 Hammer of Bogardan	1 Final Fortune
4 Incinerate	1 Firestorm
4 Shock	4 Pyroblast
	2 Shattering Pulse

Goblin Vandal

☾: Destroy target artifact defending player controls. Goblin Vandal deals no combat damage this turn. Use this ability only if Goblin Vandal is attacking and unblocked and only once each turn.

Illus. Franz Vohwinkel   1/1

Viashino Sandstalker

...talker is unaffected by ...ness.

...y turn, return Viashino ...owner's hand.

...ndstalkers to be illusions;
...now better."
...in Guide to the Desert

4/2

...haumaturgist

...: Switch power and toughness of target creature until end of turn. Effects that alter that creature's power alter its toughness instead, and vice versa, until end of turn.

Summon Dwarf

Illus. Kipling West   1/2

Mogg Flunkies

Mogg Flunkies cannot attack or block during a turn in which no other creature you control attacks or blocks.

They'll attack whatever's in front of them—as long as you tell them where that is.

Summon Goblins

Illus. Brom   3/3

BRIAN HACKER— Quarterfinalist, 1998 Worlds

Brian Hacker was the odd one out for the Worlds finals, playing a white weenie deck. His main deck was a card-for-card copy of a deck designed by Kyle Rose that Matt Linde had played the month before to win the 1998 U.S. National Championship.

"It seemed really strong, and all the deckbuilders that I talked to didn't seem to want to make any drastic changes, really any changes at all. So I decided to use the same configuration," said Hacker. "But the sideboard went through some major renovation because there was a totally different field expected at Worlds."

White weenie has been a strong **Magic** archetype since the beginning, and 1998's expansions gave it some fresh ammunition in the *en*-Kor creatures. Before the *en*-Kors, white weenie strategies were vulnerable to red creature-burn decks like Ben Rubin's (listed above). Combining a Soltari Priest's protection from red with the *en*-Kor damage redirection ability allows the Priest to, in effect, share its ability with all the *en*-Kors. There's not a lot that a mono-red deck can do in that situation. For most, the only way to destroy a creature with protection from red is Cursed Scroll…and the white deck has Disenchant, so Cursed Scroll usually becomes a single-use damage spell rather than a continuing threat.

The main strengths of Hacker's deck are its speed, the damage redirection ability of the *en*-Kors, and the Empyrial Armor–Cataclysm combination—especially when used on an unblockable protection-from-opponent's-color creature with shadow (Soltari Priest for red, Soltari Monk for black). "The ability to go second-turn shadow, third-turn Armor, fourth-turn Cataclysm is devastating against almost any deck," said Hacker. He also commented that this version "has a little bit more firepower and also a little bit more staying power than I think most white weenie decks do."

Brian Hacker's decklist

3 Nomads *en*-Kor	4 Empyrial Armor
3 Paladin *en*-Vec	4 Tithe
4 Soltari Monk	17 Plains
4 Soltari Priest	
1 Soltari Visionary	**Sideboard**
4 Soul Warden	3 Abeyance
4 Warrior *en*-Kor	2 Armageddon
4 White Knight	3 Aura of Silence
1 Aura of Silence	3 Cursed Scroll
4 Cataclysm	1 Disenchant
3 Disenchant	3 Spirit Link

RANDY BUEHLER—
12th Place, 1998 Worlds

Randy Buehler didn't quite make it into the Top 8 at Worlds, but his Standard deck was definitely one of the strongest. He designed the deck, called "CMU Blue," together with Erik Lauer, the "Mad Genius of **Magic**." The design started from the "Draw-Go" decks that placed first and second in the 1998 European Championships.

Both CMU Blue and Draw-Go are "megapermission" decks—that is, most of the spells in the deck are counter-magic. CMU Blue runs a whopping total of 21 assorted counterspells, with four more in the sideboard. Starting with the one-mana Force Spikes, the deck can potentially cast a counterspell of some sort every turn of the game. And it may need to, since it has almost

no way to deal with threats that make it past the barrage of counterspells. Unlike the more traditional blue-white or blue-red permission decks, the only card in CMU Blue's main deck that can remove a permanent is Nevinyrral's Disk. The sideboard adds a bit more permanent removal in the form of Capsize, which can remove a threat for one turn and give the counterspells another shot at it.

The European Draw-Go decks that inspired CMU Blue contained Steel Golems as their victory cards. Buehler and Lauer decided that the Golems weren't very effective against the field they expected to see at Worlds, so they looked for a different solution. Eventually they settled on Stalking Stones plus a single Rainbow Efreet. The Efreet's phasing ability makes it very difficult for an opponent without

countermagic to get rid of, and Stalking Stones is immune to counter-magic, so between the two they cover all bases.

The CMU Blue deck's strategy is to take control of the game, countering everything that could pose a threat (or using the Disk against threats that make it past the counterspells) while building up a large mana base. Once the player has enough land, he or she can start playing Whispers of the Muse with buyback at the end of the opponent's turn. Those extra draws provide enough countermagic ammunition to counter everything. Then a Nevinyrral's Disk can clear the board and countermagic can keep it clear, allowing a single Rainbow Efreet or animated Stalking Stones to waltz across enough times to finish off the opponent.

Randy Buehler's decklist

1 Rainbow Efreet	4 Nevinyrral's Disk
4 Counterspell	18 Island
4 Dismiss	4 Quicksand
2 Dissipate	4 Stalking Stones
3 Forbid	
4 Force Spike	**Sideboard**
4 Impulse	2 Capsize
3 Mana Leak	1 Grindstone
1 Memory Lapse	4 Hydroblast
4 Whispers of the Muse	4 Sea Sprite
	4 Wasteland

Nevinyrral's Disk comes into play tapped.

1, ⊙: Destroy all artifacts, creatures, and enchantments.

Buyback 5 (*You may pay an additional 5 when you play this spell. If you do, put it into your hand instead of your graveyard as part of the spell's effect.*)

Draw a card.

"I followed her song only to find it was
—Crovax

Flying

⟨⟩⟨⟩: Phase out

"A beauty made more so by its fleeting visitations."
—Teferi

3/1

⊙: Add one colorless mana to your mana pool.

6: Stalking Stones becomes a 3/3 artifact creature permanently. (*This creature still counts as a land.*)

Card 1 — 1RR

ECHO BOOM

ENCHANTMENT

ECHO

WHEN ECHO BOOM COMES INTO PLAY, DESTROY TARGET LAND

WHEN THE ECHO COST IS PAID, RETURN ECHO BOOM TO ITS OWNER'S HAND

Card 2 — 4BBB

RABID CHIHUAHUA

CREATURE — HOUND

R.C. can't be blocked except by artifact and black creatures. At the beginning of your upkeep, put a venom counter on R.C. Whenever R.C. deals damage to a player, that player recieves poison counters equal to the number of venom counters on R.C.

6: Regenerate R C

3/3

Card 3 — 1U

PSYCHIC FRIENDS

ENCHANTMENT

YOU MAY LOOK AT THE CARDS IN YOUR LIBRARY WITHOUT CHANGING THEIR ORDER.

Card 4 — 2G

IT'S ALL ABOUT ME

ENCHANTMENT

STATIC ABILITIES ON ARTIFACTS AND GLOBAL ENCHANTMENTS AFFECT ONLY YOU AND CREATURES YOU CONTROL.

Card 5 — 1

BETHMO'S BANE

ARTIFACT

TAPPED PERMANENTS LOSE ALL OF THEIR ABILITIES.

Card 6 — 2GG

ECHO LORD

CREATURE — LORD

ECHO.

CREATURES WITH ECHO GET +2/+2 AND LOSE ECHO.

2/3

SAMPLE PLAYTEST CARDS

When a **Magic: The Gathering** expansion is designed, many card concepts that don't make it into the final set are tested. By testing more cards than are needed, the design team leaves leeway for cutting cards, making sure that the expansion is well balanced and that all the cards in it are playable, useful, and entertaining. Playtest cards that don't make it into an expansion are usually broken or otherwise unsuitable. The cards above are examples of ideas that didn't make it through the testing processes for the expansions in this encyclopedia.

DECKBUILDERS' INDEXES

LANDWALKING CREATURES

PLAINSWALK
Righteous Avengers

FORESTWALK
Cat Warriors
Eladamri, Lord of Leaves
Erhnam Djinn
Heartwood Treefolk
Mirri, Cat Warrior
Rime Dryad
Scarwood Bandits
Scarwood Hag
Shanodin Dryads
Unseen Walker
Veldrane of Sengir
Weatherseed Elf
Wormwood Treefolk

MOUNTAINWALK
Canyon Wildcat
Cave People
Dwarven Pony
Enslaved Scout
Goblin King
Goblin Scouts
Goblin Spelunkers
Goblins of the Flarg
Mountain Goat
Mountain Yeti
River Merfolk
Vug Lizard

SWAMPWALK
Anaconda
Bayou Dragonfly
Bog Raiders
Bog Wraith
Dirtwater Wraith
Funeral Charm
Legions of Lim-Dûl
Marsh Goblins
Moor Fiend
Odylic Wraith
Plague Beetle
Pygmy Allosaurus
Sol'kanar the Swamp King
Urborg
Warthog
Witch Engine
Zombie Master

ISLANDWALK
Benthic Behemoth
Benthic Djinn
Bull Hippo
Goblin Flotilla
Lord of Atlantis
Merfolk Assassin
Merfolk Raiders
Pale Bears
River Boa
Segovian Leviathan
War Barge

REGENERATING CREATURES
Albino Troll

Baron Sengir
Bone Shaman
Cadaverous Knight
Carnassid
Clay Statue
Clergy of the Holy Nimbus
Clockwork Gnomes
Clot Sliver
Dark Hatchling
Drudge Skeletons
Eron the Relentless
Feral Thallid
Fog of Gnats
Ghost Ship
Goblin Chirurgeon
Gorilla Chieftain
Hurr Jackal
Khabál Ghoul
Kjeldoran Dead
Krakilin
Lich
Lim-Dûl's Cohort
Lim-Dûl's High Guard
Living Wall
Locust Swarm
Lord of Tresserhorn
Matopi Golem
Mischievous Poltergeist
Niall Silvain
Nurturing Licid
Orcish Healer
Orcish Mechanics
Patchwork Gnomes
Pit Trap
Priest of Yawgmoth
Pygmy Troll
Ragnar
Ranger en-Vec
Restless Dead
River Boa
Rootwater Alligator
Sage of Lat-Nam
Sanguine Guard
Scavenging Ghoul
Screeching Harpy
Sea Troll
Sedge Troll
Seedling Charm
Skeleton Scavengers
Skyshroud Troll
Soldevi Sentry
Soldevi Steam Beast
Spawning Pool
Spike Hatcher
Spined Fluke
Spiny Starfish
The Brute
Thrull Retainer
Uktabi Wildcats
Unworthy Dead
Uthden Troll
Vigilant Martyr
Vile Requiem
Village Elder
Wake of Vultures
Walking Dead
Wall of Bone
Wall of Brambles
Wall of Pine Needles
Whippoorwill

Will-O'-The-Wisp
Winds of Rath
Yavimaya Gnats
Yawgmoth Demon
Zombie Master
zombie scavengers

BANDING CREATURES
Adventurers' Guildhouse
Ayesha Tanaka
Baton of Morale
Battering Ram
Beast Walkers
Benalish Hero
Benalish Infantry
Camel
Cathedral of Serra
Cooperation
Dire Wolves
Errand of Duty
Formation
Fortified Area
Helm of Chatzuk
Icatian Infantry
Icatian Phalanx
Icatian Skirmishers
Kjeldoran Escort
Kjeldoran Knight
Kjeldoran Phalanx
Kjeldoran Skycaptain
Kjeldoran Skyknight
Kjeldoran Warrior
Knights of Thorn
Master of the Hunt
Mesa Pegasus
Mishra's War Machine
Mountain Stronghold
Nalathni Dragon
Nature's Blessing
Noble Elephant
Pikemen
Seafarers' Quay
Shelkin Brownie
Shield Bearer
Soraya the Falconer
Teremko Griffin
Timber Wolves
Tolaria
Unholy Citadel
Urza's Avenger
Urza's Engine
Volunteer Reserves
Wall of Caltrops
Wall of Shields
War Elephant

BOOSTING/PUMPABLE CREATURES
Acidic Sliver
Anaba Spirit Crafter
Armor Sliver
Barbed Sliver
Bone Shaman
Citanul Hierophants
Clot Sliver
Deranged Hermit
Eladamri, Lord of Leaves
Faerie Noble
Giant Albatross
Goblin Flotilla
Goblin King

Goblin Soothsayer
Grollub
Hibernation Sliver
Horned Sliver
Icatian Skirmishers
Ivory Guardians
Jacques le Vert
Johan
Juniper Order Advocate
Kaysa
Knight of Valor
Kobold Drill Sergeant
Kobold Overlord
Kobold Taskmaster
Lord of Atlantis
Márton Stromgald
Mindwhip Sliver
Mnemonic Sliver
Muscle Sliver
Rank and File
Renegade Warlord
Rogue Skycaptain
Rohgahh of Kher Keep
Soltari Champion
Soraya the Falconer
Spike Cannibal
Spined Sliver
Spitting Slug
Stronghold Taskmaster
Talon Sliver
Telim'Tor
Thrull Champion
Victual Sliver
Watchdog
Winged Sliver
Zombie Master
Zuberi, Golden Feather

CREATURES WITH FLANKING
Barbed Foliage
Burning Shield Askari
Cadaverous Knight
Fallen Askari
Femeref Knight
Jabari's Banner
Jolrael's Centaur
Knight of the Mists
Knight of Valor
Mtenda Herder
Searing Spear Askari
Shadow Rider
Sidar Jabari
Suq'Ata Lancer
Teferi's Honor Guard
Telim'Tor
Zhalfirin Commander
Zhalfirin Crusader
Zhalfirin Knight

CREATURES WITH FLYING

Black
Abyssal Horror
Abyssal Specter
Baron Sengir
Bellowing Fiend
Bog Imp
Bone Shredder
Catacomb Dragon
Circling Vultures

Crazed Skirge
Dark Hatchling
Entropic Specter
Fallen Angel
Feral Shadow
Fledgling Djinn
Fog of Gnats
Hyalopterous Lemure
Hypnotic Specter
Junún Efreet
Lord of the Pit
Maddening Imp
Mischievous Poltergeist
Morinfen
Nightmare
Phyrexian Debaser
Pit Imp
Ravenous Skirge
Ravenous Vampire
Revenant
Screeching Harpy
Sengir Bats
Sengir Vampire
Shauku, Endbringer
Skirge Familiar
Skittering Skirge
Skulking Ghost
Skyshroud Vampire
Spirit of the Night
Swamp Mosquito
Tainted Specter
Tethered Skirge
Vampire Bats
Wake of Vultures
Will-O'-The-Wisp
Yawgmoth Demon

Blue
Air Elemental
Avizoa
Azimaet Drake
Azure Drake
Bay Falcon
Breezekeeper
Cerulean Wyvern
Cloud Djinn
Cloud Elemental
Cloud Spirit
Cloud of Faeries
Drifting Djinn
Ephemeron
Fighting Drake
Fleeting Image
Flying Men
Fog Bank
Fog Elemental
Fylamarid
Ghost Ship
Giant Albatross
Gilded Drake
Hakim, Loreweaver
Harmattan Efreet
Illusionary Forces
Illusionary Wall
Mahamoti Djinn
Mawcor
Mirozel
Mist Dragon
Palinchron

Pendrell Drake
Peregrine Drake
Phantasmal Forces
Phantasmal Mount
Phantasmal Sphere
Phantom Monster
Rainbow Efreet
Raven Familiar
Sage Owl
Sea Sprite
Serendib Djinn
Serendib Efreet
Shimmering Efreet
Shrieking Drake
Sibilant Spirit
Silver Erne
Silver Wyvern
Skyshroud Condor
Somnophore
Spindrift Drake
Spire Owl
Storm Crow
Storm Elemental
Teferi's Drake
Teferi's Imp
Thornwind Faeries
Thunder Wall
Timid Drake
Tolarian Drake
Tradewind Rider
Vaporous Djinn
Vigilant Drake
Vodalian Knights
Wall of Air
Waterspout Djinn
Wayward Soul
Weatherseed Faeries
Wind Dancer
Wind Drake
Wind Spirit
Zephid
Zephyr Falcon

Red
Bird Maiden
Bogardan Phoenix
Canyon Drake
Crimson Hellkite
Crimson Manticore
Crimson Roc
Dragon Whelp
Emberwilde Djinn
Fire Drake
Firefly
Firestorm Phoenix
Flowstone Wyvern
Goblin Balloon Brigade
Goblin Ski Patrol
Granite Gargoyle
Lightning Dragon
Nalathni Dragon
Rathi Dragon
Roc of Kher Ridges
Rogue Skycaptain
Sabertooth Wyvern
Shard Phoenix
Shivan Dragon
Shivan Hellkite
Shivan Phoenix

Spitting Drake
Volcanic Dragon
Green
Bayou Dragonfly
Birds of Paradise
Canopy Dragon
Cockatrice
Emerald Dragonfly
Faerie Noble
Fire Sprites
Flailing Drake
Hawkeater Moth
Ifh-Biff Efreet
Killer Bees
Kyscu Drake
Leaping Lizard
Locust Swarm
Mindbender Spores
Pixie Queen
Scryb Sprites
Uktabi Faerie
Willow Faerie
Yavimaya Gnats

White
Abbey Gargoyles
Alabaster Dragon
Angelic Curator
Angelic Page
Angelic Protector
Archangel
Armored Pegasus
Avenging Angel
Carrier Pigeons
Cloudchaser Eagle
Daraja Griffin
Duskrider Falcon
Ekundu Griffin
Exalted Dragon
Freewind Falcon
Herald of Serra
Ivory Gargoyle
Karmic Guide
Melesse Spirit
Mesa Falcon
Mesa Pegasus
Mistmoon Griffin
Mtenda Griffin
Osai Vultures
Pearl Dragon
Pegasus Charger
Radiant, Archangel
Seraph
Serra Angel
Skyshroud Falcon
Spirit en-Kor
Sunweb
Sustainer of the Realm
Thunder Spirit
Unyaro Griffin
Voice of Grace
Voice of Law
Wall of Resistance
Wall of Swords
Warrior Angel
Welkin Hawk
Wild Aesthir
Zuberi, Golden Feather

Gold
Arcades Sabboth
Asmira, Holy Avenger
Chromium
Dracoplasm
Emberwilde Caliph
Firestorm Hellkite
Frenetic Efreet
Guiding Spirit
Haunting Apparition
Hazerider Drake
Leering Gargoyle
Nicol Bolas
Palladia-Mors
Phelddagrif
Sawback Manticore
Selenia, Dark Angel
Sky Spirit
Storm Spirit
Tempest Drake
Tuknir Deathlock
Vaevictis Asmadi
Viashivan Dragon
Windreaper Falcon
Xira Arien

Artifacts
Aesthir Glider
Clockwork Avian
Dancing Scimitar
Flying Carpet
Ornithopter
Patagia Golem
Roterothopter
Teeka's Dragon
Tetravus
Thopter Squadron
Tin-Wing Chimera

CREATURES THAT ARE HARD TO BLOCK, BUT DO NOT LANDWALK
Argothian Pixies
Basalt Golem
Bog Rats
Bouncing Beebles
Breezekeeper
Charging Rhino
Cloak of Invisibility
Clockwork Steed
Clockwork Swarm
Commander Greven il-Vec
Corrupting Licid
Dauthi Horror
Dream Prowler
Dwarven Nomad
Dwarven Warriors
Elder Spawn
Elven Riders
Ertai's Familiar
Flow of Maggots
Fylamarid
Goblin Sappers
Gorilla Berserkers
Katabatic Winds
Manta Ray
Marsh Lurker
Merfolk Raiders
Order of Yawgmoth
Phantom Warrior

Phyrexian Colossus
Razortooth Rats
Sandbar Crocodile
Searing Spear Askari
Shimmer
Shimmering Efreet
Stalking Tiger
Stone Spirit
Suq'Ata Assassin
Taniwha
Teferi's Curse
Teferi's Drake
Teferi's Imp
Time and Tide
Tolarian Drake
Treetop Rangers
Varchild's Crusader
Viashino Runner
Walking Dream
Warping Wurm
Wind Spirit

CREATURES WITH PHASING

Breezekeeper
Cloak of Invisibility
Ertai's Familiar
Katabatic Winds
Merfolk Raiders
Sandbar Crocodile
Shimmer
Shimmering Efreet
Taniwha
Teferi's Curse
Teferi's Drake
Teferi's Imp
Teferi's Isle
Time and Tide
Tolarian Drake
Warping Wurm

POISONOUS CREATURES

Serpent Generator
Leeches
Marsh Viper
Sabertooth Cobra
Crypt Cobra
Pit Scorpion
Suq'Ata Assassin
Swamp Mosquito

CARDS THAT HAVE OR GRANT PROTECTION

FROM BLACK

Black
Cemetery Gate
Minion of Leshrac
Spirit of the Night

Green
Darkwatch Elves
Whirling Dervish
Willow Priestess

White
Absolute Grace
Black Ward

Death Speakers
Disciple of Grace
Duskrider Falcon
Karmic Guide
Melesse Spirit
Order of Leitbur
Order of the White Shield
Paladin en-Vec
Soltari Monk
Voice of Grace
Wall of Light
White Knight

Gold
Righteous War
Scalebane's Elite

FROM BLUE

Green
Bloated Toad
Karoo Meerkat
Scragnoth

Red
Guma

White
Blue Ward

Gold
Windreaper Falcon

FROM GREEN

Blue
Cerulean Wyvern

White
Green Ward

FROM RED

Blue
Narwhal
Sea Sprite
Weatherseed Faeries

Red
Beasts of Bogardan
Keeper of Kookus
Subterranean Spirit

White
Abbey Gargoyles
Absolute Law
Defender of Law
Disciple of Law
Freewind Falcon
Ivory Guardians
Knights of Thorn
Paladin en-Vec
Red Ward
Repentant Blacksmith
Soltari Priest
Voice of Law

Gold
Hazerider Drake

FROM WHITE

Black
Black Knight
Eviscerator
Ihsan's Shade
Knight of Stromgald
Order of the Ebon Hand
Wall of Putrid Flesh

Red
Defender of Chaos
Goblin Wizard
Mountain Yeti
Wildfire Emissary

White
White Ward

Gold
Righteous War

FROM ARTIFACTS

Green
Yavimaya Scion

White
Angelic Curator

CREATURES WITH A PROTECTION

Black
Black Knight
Cemetery Gate
Eviscerator
Ihsan's Shade
Knight of Stromgald
Minion of Leshrac
Order of the Ebon Hand
Spirit of the Night
Wall of Putrid Flesh

Blue
Cerulean Wyvern
Escaped Shapeshifter
Narwhal
Sea Sprite
Weatherseed Faeries

Green
Bloated Toad
Darkwatch Elves
Karoo Meerkat
Scragnoth
Whirling Dervish
Willow Priestess
Yavimaya Scion

Red
Beasts of Bogardan
Defender of Chaos
Goblin Wizard
Guma
Keeper of Kookus
Mountain Yeti
Subterranean Spirit
Wildfire Emissary

White
Abbey Gargoyles
Angelic Curator
Death Speakers
Defender of Law
Disciple of Grace
Disciple of Law
Duskrider Falcon
Freewind Falcon
Ivory Guardians
Karmic Guide
Knight of Dawn
Knights of Thorn
Melesse Spirit
Mother of Runes
Order of Leitbur
Order of the White Shield
Paladin en-Vec
Repentant Blacksmith
Soltari Monk
Soltari Priest
Voice of Grace
Voice of Law
Wall of Light
White Knight

Gold
Hazerider Drake
Scalebane's Elite
Windreaper Falcon

CREATURES WITH RAMPAGE

Horrible Hordes
Teeka's Dragon
Chromium
Gabriel Angelfire
Hunding Gjornersen
Marhault Elsdragon
Rapid Fire
Craw Giant
Gorilla Berserkers
Wolverine Pack
Ærathi Berserker
Balduvian War-Makers
Frost Giant
Varchild's War-Riders

CREATURES THAT DO NOT TAP ON ATTACK

Angel's Trumpet
Archangel
Ardent Militia
Bartel Runeaxe
Bay Falcon
Eternal Warrior
Femeref Knight
Ghost Hounds
Iron-Heart Chimera
Mirri, Cat Warrior
Opal Archangel
Rabid Wombat
Radiant, Archangel
Serra Angel
Serra Paladin
Serra's Blessing
Serra's Embrace
Skyshroud Falcon
Standing Troops
Tempest Drake

DECKBUILDERS' INDEXES

Windseeker Centaur
Yotian Soldier
Zephyr Falcon

CREATURES WITH TRAMPLE

Black
Aku Djinn
Black Carriage
Ebon Praetor
Gallowbraid
Minion of the Wastes
Nameless Race

Blue
Deep Spawn
Giant Shark
Leviathan
Polar Kraken

Red
Ball Lightning
Flowstone Mauler
Goblin Mutant
Goblin Rock Sled
Kobold Drill Sergeant
Kookus
Orgg
Two-Headed Giant of Foriys
Varchild's War-Riders

Green
Argothian Swine
Argothian Wurm
Aurochs
Berserk
Canopy Dragon
Carnassid
Child of Gaea
Cradle Guard
Crash of Rhinos
Craw Giant
Endless Wurm
Force of Nature
Gorilla Berserkers
Rootbreaker Wurm
Skyshroud War Beast
Stampeding Wildebeests
War Mammoth
Weatherseed Treefolk
Wild Elephant
Yavimaya Ants
Yavimaya Wurm

White
Angry Mob
Elder Land Wurm
Iron Tusk Elephant
Lancers en-Kor
Moorish Cavalry
War Elephant

Gold
Axelrod Gunnarson
Gabriel Angelfire
Lim-Dûl's Paladin
Palladia-Mors
Phelddagrif

Artifact s
Bronze Horse
Colossus of Sardia
Ebony Rhino
Igneous Golem
Lead-Belly Chimera
Phyrexian Dreadnought
Urza's Engine Wild Elephant
Woolly Mammoths
Xanthic Statue
Yavimaya Ants
Yavimaya Wurm

TOKEN GENERATORS

Afterlife
Balduvian Dead
Basalt Golem
Boris Devilboon
Bottle of Suleiman
Breeding Pit
Broken Visage
Caribou Range
Carrion
Cyclopean Tomb
Dance of Many
Deranged Hermit
Diamond Kaleidoscope
Drudge Spell
Echo Chamber
Elvish Farmer
Errand of Duty
Feast or Famine
Field of Souls
Giant Caterpillar
Goblin Offensive
Goblin Scouts
Goblin Warrens
Greener Pastures
Hazezon Tamar
Homarid Spawning Bed
Hornet Cannon
Icatian Town
Jungle Patrol
Keeper of the Beasts
Kjeldoran Home Guard
Kjeldoran Outpost
Lab Rats
Liege of the Hollows
Master of the Hunt
Metrognome
Midsummer Revel
Mogg Infestation
Mongrel Pack
Night Soil
Ovinomancer
Pegasus Refuge
Pegasus Stampede
Phantasmal Sphere
Phelddagrif
Phyrexian Processor
Sacred Mesa
Sarcomancy
Sengir Autocrat
Serpent Generator
Sliver Queen
Snake Basket
Spike Breeder
Spiny Starfish
Spirit Mirror

Splintering Wind
Sporogenesis
Stangg
Tetravus
Thallid
Thallid Devourer
The Hive
Thopter Squadron
Tidal Wave
Tombstone Stairwell
Tooth and Claw
Varchild's War-Riders
Verdant Force
Volrath's Laboratory
Waiting in the Weeds
Wall of Kelp
Waylay

LEGENDS

Adun Oakenshield
Angus Mackenzie
Arcades Sabboth
Asmira, Holy Avenger
Autumn Willow
Axelrod Gunnarson
Ayesha Tanaka
Barktooth Warbeard
Baron Sengir
Barrin, Master Wizard
Bartel Runeaxe
Boris Devilboon
Chandler
Chromium
Commander Greven il-Vec
Crovax The Cursed
Dakkon Blackblade
Daughter of Autumn
Eladamri, Lord of Leaves
Eron the Relentless
Ertai, Wizard Adept
Gabriel Angelfire
Gallowbraid
General Jarkeld
Gosta Dirk
Grandmother Sengir
Gwendlyn Di Corci
Hakim, Loreweaver
Halfdane
Hazduhr the Abbot
Hazezon Tamar
Hivis of the Scale
Hunding Gjornersen
Ihsan's Shade
Irini Sengir
Jacques le Vert
Jasmine Boreal
Jedit Ojanen
Johan
Joven
Kasimir the Lone Wolf
Kaysa
Kei Takahashi
Lady Caleria
Lady Evangela
Lady Orca
Livonya Silone
Lord Magnus
Lord of Tresserhorn

Maraxus of Keld
Marhault Elsdragon
Márton Stromgald
Merieke Ri Berit
Mirri, Cat Warrior
Morinfen
Multani, Maro-Sorcerer
Nebuchadnezzar
Nicol Bolas
Orim, Samite Healer
Palladia-Mors
Pavel Maliki
Phelddagrif
Princess Lucrezia
Purraj of Urborg
Radiant, Archangel
Ragnar
Ramirez DePietro
Ramses Overdark
Rashida Scalebane
Rashka the Slayer
Rasputin Dreamweaver
Reveka, Wizard Savant
Riven Turnbull
Rohgahh of Kher Keep
Rubinia Soulsinger
Selenia, Dark Angel
Shauku, Endbringer
Sidar Jabari
Sir Shandlar of Eberyn
Sivitri Scarzam
Skeleton Ship
Sliver Queen
Sol'kanar the Swamp King
Soraya the Falconer
Spirit of the Night
Stangg
Starke of Rath
Sunastian Falconer
Taniwha
Telim'Tor
Tetsuo Umezawa
The Lady of the Mountain
Tobias Andrion
Tor Wauki
Torsten von Ursus
Tuknir Deathlock
Ur-Drago
Vaevictis Asmadi
Veldrane of Sengir
Vhati il-Dal
Xira Arien
Zirilan of the Claw
Zuberi, Golden Feather

CANTRIPS

Black
Bone Harvest
Fevered Strength
Gravebind
Headstone
Krovikan Fetish
Krovikan Plague
Mind Ravel
Soul Rend
Touch of Death
Vampirism

Caravan
Trade Caravan

Carriage
Black Carriage

Carrier
Phyrexian Debaser
Phyrexian Defiler
Phyrexian Denouncer
Phyrexian Plaguelord

Cat
Canyon Wildcat
Cave Tiger
Guma
Pouncing Jaguar

Cat Warriors
Cat Warriors
Panther Warriors

Caterpillar
Giant Caterpillar

Cavalry
Moorish Cavalry

Cave People
Cave People

Centaur
Centaur Archer
Jolrael's Centaur
Windseeker Centaur

Centaurs
Citanul Centaurs

Cheetah
King Cheetah

Cleric
Abbey Matron
Balduvian Shaman
Benalish Missionary
Blighted Shaman
Brine Shaman
Clergy en-Vec
Disciple of Grace
Disciple of Law
Elder Druid
Elvish Healer
Faith Healer
Farrelite Priest
Femeref Healer
Frevalise Supplicant
Icatian Priest
Juniper Order Druid
Ley Druid
Monk Idealist
Monk Realist
Mother of Runes
Noble Benefactor
Orcish Healer
Priest of Yawgmoth
Royal Herbalist
Sacred Guide
Samite Healer

Sanctum Custodian
Shaman en-Kor
Silent Attendant
Soldevi Adnate
Soltari Monk
Soltari Priest
Soltari Visionary
Songstitcher
Soul Shepherd
Soul Warden
Storm Shaman
Sylvan Hierophant
Thelonite Druid
Thelonite Monk
Venerable Monk
Wandering Mage

Clerics
Initiates of the Ebon Hand
Order of Leitbur
Order of the Ebon Hand

Clone
Clone

Cobra
Crypt Cobra
Hornet Cobra
Sabertooth Cobra

Cockatrice
Cockatrice

Constable
An-Havva Constable

Crab
Giant Crab
Horseshoe Crab
King Crab

Crocodile
Sandbar Crocodile

Crusader
Aysen Crusader

Cyclops
Bloodrock Cyclops
Ekundu Cyclops
Hulking Cyclops
Tar Pit Warrior

Dandán
Dandán

Dead
Kjeldoran Dead

Demon
Lord of the Pit
Minion of Leshrac
Minion of Tevesh Szat
Yawgmoth Demon

Demons
Demonic Hordes

Dervish
Whirling Dervish

Devils
Stone-Throwing Devils

Devouring Deep
Devouring Deep

Dinosaur
Pygmy Allosaurus

Djinn
Aku Djinn
Benthic Djinn
Breezekeeper
Cloud Djinn
Drifting Djinn
Emberwilde Caliph
Emberwilde Djinn
Erhnam Djinn
Fledgling Djinn
Juzám Djinn
Kookus
Mahamoti Djinn
Mijae Djinn
Nettletooth Djinn
Serendib Djinn
Vaporous Djinn
Waterspout Djinn

Dog
Snow Hound

Doppelganger
Vesuvan Doppelganger

Dragon
Alabaster Dragon
Canopy Dragon
Catacomb Dragon
Crimson Hellkite
Dragon Whelp
Exalted Dragon
Firestorm Hellkite
Lightning Dragon
Mist Dragon
Nalathni Dragon
Pearl Dragon
Rathi Dragon
Shivan Dragon
Shivan Hellkite
Viashivan Dragon
Volcanic Dragon

Dragonfly
Emerald Dragonfly

Drake
Azimaet Drake
Azure Drake
Canyon Drake
Fighting Drake
Fire Drake
Flailing Drake
Flowstone Wyvern
Gilded Drake
Hazerider Drake
Kyscu Drake

Pendrell Drake
Peregrine Drake
Sabertooth Wyvern
Shrieking Drake
Silver Wyvern
Spindrift Drake
Spitting Drake
Teferi's Drake
Tempest Drake
Timid Drake
Tolarian Drake
Vigilant Drake
Wind Drake

Drill Sergeant
Kobold Drill Sergeant

Druid
Avenging Druid
Citanul Druid
Fugitive Druid
Fyndhorn Druid
Hermit Druid
Ichneumon Druid
Quirion Druid
Village Elder
Wood Sage

Druids
Citanul Hierophants

Dryad
Heartwood Dryad
Rime Dryad
Unseen Walker

Dryads
Folk of the Pines

Dwarf
Dwarven Armorer
Dwarven Berserker
Dwarven Lieutenant
Dwarven Miner
Dwarven Nomad
Dwarven Soldier
Dwarven Thaumaturgist
Dwarven Trader

Dwarves
Dwarven Demolition Team
Dwarven Sea Clan
Dwarven Vigilantes
Dwarven Warriors
Dwarven Weaponsmith

Eater
Eater of the Dead

Eel
Electric Eel

Effigy
Blazing Effigy

Efreet
Burning Palm Efreet
Frenetic Efreet
Harmattan Efreet

Ifh-Biff Efreet
Junún Efreet
Rainbow Efreet
Serendib Efreet
Shimmering Efreet
Tempest Efreet
Uktabi Efreet
Wildfire Emissary
Ydwen Efreet

Egg
Rukh Egg

El-Hajjâj
El-Hajjâj

Elder Dragon Legend
Arcades Sabboth
Chromium
Nicol Bolas
Palladia-Mors
Vaevictis Asmadi

Elemental
Air Elemental
Child of Gaea
Cloud Elemental
Earth Elemental
Fire Elemental
Flame Elemental
Fog Elemental
Fungus Elemental
Lightning Elemental
Magmasaur
Storm Elemental
Subterranean Spirit
Time Elemental
Verdant Force
Water Elemental
Wave Elemental
Wood Elemental

Elementals
Furnace Brood

Elephant
Bull Elephant
Crazed Armodon
Endangered Armodon
Iron Tusk Elephant
Noble Elephant
Rogue Elephant
Trained Armodon
Trumpeting Armodon
War Elephant
Wild Elephant

Elf
Argothian Elder
Deranged Hermit
Elvish Bard
Elvish Berserker
Elvish Farmer
Elvish Herder
Elvish Hunter
Elvish Lyrist
Elvish Ranger
Elvish Scout
Fyndhorn Elder

Llanowar Druid
Llanowar Sentinel
Multani's Acolyte
Priest of Titania
Quirion Ranger
Seeker of Skybreak
Skyshroud Archer
Skyshroud Elf
Skyshroud Ranger
Titania's Chosen
Weatherseed Elf
Yavimaya Granger

Elves
Darkwatch Elves
Elves of Deep Shadow
Elvish Archers
Fyndhorn Elves
Llanowar Elves
Quirion Elves
Savaen Elves
Skyshroud Elite
Skyshroud Troopers
Treetop Rangers
Wood Elves

Enchantress
Argothian Enchantress
Femeref Enchantress
Verduran Enchantress

Entity
Psionic Entity

Erne
Silver Erne

Evil Eye
Evil Eye of Orms-By-Gore

Exorcist
Exorcist

Faerie
Aisling Leprechaun
Sea Sprite
Shelkin Brownie
Uktabi Faerie
Willow Faerie
Willow Priestess
Wind Dancer

Faeries
Argothian Pixies
Cloud of Faeries
Fire Sprites
Scryb Sprites
Thornwind Faeries
Weatherseed Faeries

Falcon
Bay Falcon
Duskrider Falcon
Freewind Falcon
Mesa Falcon
Windreaper Falcon
Zephyr Falcon

Fallen
The Fallen

Ferrets
Joven's Ferrets

Fiend
Moor Fiend

Fiends
Timmerian Fiends

Fish
Hammerhead Shark
Manta Ray
School of Piranha

Flying Men
Flying Men

Folk Of An-Havva
Folk of An-Havva

Force
Force of Nature

Foxes
Arctic Foxes

Frog
Whiptongue Frog

Frostbeast
Kjeldoran Frostbeast

Fungus
Feral Thallid
Spore Flower
Thallid
Thallid Devourer
Thorn Thallid

Fungusaur
Fungusaur

Gaea's Avenger
Gaea's Avenger

Gaea's Liege
Gaea's Liege

Gargoyle
Granite Gargoyle
Ivory Gargoyle
Leering Gargoyle

Gargoyles
Abbey Gargoyles

Gatekeeper
Abyssal Gatekeeper

General
Orc General

Ghost/s
Anaba Ancestor
Ghosts of the Damned
Haunting Apparition

Mischievous Poltergeist
Skulking Ghost

Ghoul
Ashen Ghoul
Khabál Ghoul
Scavenging Ghoul

Giant
Bone Shaman
Cinder Giant
Craven Giant
Craw Giant
Flowstone Giant
Frost Giant
Heartwood Giant
Hill Giant
Karplusan Giant
Lowland Giant
Marble Titan
Skyshroud Troll
Stone Giant
Thundering Giant
Tor Giant
Two-Headed Giant of Foriys

Gnomes
Quarum Trench Gnomes

Goat
Mountain Goat

Goblin/s
Enslaved Scout
Goblin Artisans
Goblin Balloon Brigade
Goblin Cadets
Goblin Chirurgeon
Goblin Digging Team
Goblin Elite Infantry
Goblin Flotilla
Goblin Grenadiers
Goblin Hero
Goblin Lackey
Goblin Matron
Goblin Medics
Goblin Mutant
Goblin Patrol
Goblin Raider
Goblin Recruiter
Goblin Sappers
Goblin Ski Patrol
Goblin Snowman
Goblin Soothsayer
Goblin Spelunkers
Goblin Swine-Rider
Goblin Tinkerer
Goblin Vandal
Goblin War Buggy
Goblin Welder
Goblin Wizard
Goblins of the Flarg
Keeper of Kookus
Marsh Goblins
Mogg Assassin
Mogg Bombers
Mogg Conscripts
Mogg Fanatic
Mogg Flunkies

DECKBUILDERS' INDEXES

Mogg Maniac
Mogg Raider
Mogg Squad
Mons's Goblin Raiders
Okk
Raging Goblin
Scarwood Goblins

Gorilla
Gargantuan Gorilla
Gorilla Chieftain
Gorilla Shaman
Raging Gorilla

Gorilla Pack
Gorilla Pack

Gorillas
Gorilla Berserkers

Gremlins
Phyrexian Gremlins

Griffin
Daraja Griffin
Ekundu Griffin
Mistmoon Griffin
Mtenda Griffin
Teremko Griffin
Unyaro Griffin

Guardian
Guardian Beast
Harbor Guardian
Spectral Guardian
Sustaining Spirit

Guardians
Ivory Guardians

Gypsies
Pradesh Gypsies

Hag
Brine Hag
Scarwood Hag

Harlequin
Chaos Harlequin

Hell's Caretaker
Hell's Caretaker

Heretic
Soldevi Heretic

Hero
Benalish Hero
Kjeldoran Warrior

Heroes
Beast Walkers

Hipparion
Hipparion

Hippo
Bull Hippo

Hippopotamus
Pygmy Hippo

Homarid
Deep Spawn
Homarid
Homarid Shaman
Homarid Warrior
Viscerid Drone

Horror
Abyssal Horror
Cosmic Horror
Dark Hatchling
Eviscerator
Flesh Reaver
Krovikan Horror
Spined Fluke
Vebulid
Witch Engine

Horseman
Headless Horseman

Hound
Dauthi Jackal
Jackal Pup
Monstrous Hound

Hounds
Elven Warhounds
Ghost Hounds
Hollow Dogs
Lava Hounds
Mongrel Pack
Vampire Hounds
Wild Dogs

Hunter
Abyssal Hunter
Witch Hunter

Hydra
Balduvian Hydra
Molten Hydra
Rock Hydra
Spitting Hydra

Hyenas
Gibbering Hyenas

Illusion
Dream Prowler
Ephemeron
Ertai's Familiar
Fleeting Image
Illusionary Forces
Illusionary Presence
Imaginary Pet
Mirozel
Palinchron
Phantom Warrior
Somnophore
Thalakos Mistfolk
Walking Dream
Zephid

Imp
Bog Imp

Crazed Skirge
Foul Imp
Maddening Imp
Nettling Imp
Norritt
Pit Imp
Ravenous Skirge
Skirge Familiar
Skittering Skirge
Teferi's Imp
Tethered Skirge

Infernal Denizen
Infernal Denizen

Inquisitors
Serra Inquisitors

Insect
Acridian
Bayou Dragonfly
Deadly Insect
Duct Crawler
Firefly
Giant Cockroach
Hawkeater Moth
Plague Beetle
Shocker

Insects
Army Ants
Brood of Cockroaches
Carrion Beetles
Fire Ants
Flow of Maggots
Fog of Gnats
Mind Maggots
Pincher Beetles
Yavimaya Gnats

Island Fish
Island Fish Jasconius

Jackal
Hurr Jackal

Jellyfish
Man-o'-War

Keeper
Keeper of Tresserhorn

Keepers
Keepers of the Faith

King
King Suleiman

Kithkin
Amrou Kithkin

Knight
Agent of Stromgald
Benalish Knight
Black Knight
Burning Shield Askari
Cadaverous Knight
Charging Paladin
Dauthi Mercenary

Defender of Chaos
Defender of Law
Eastern Paladin
Fallen Askari
Femeref Knight
Juniper Order Advocate
Kjeldoran Knight
Knight of Dawn
Knight of Dusk
Knight of Stromgald
Knight of Valor
Knight of the Mists
Order of Yawgmoth
Paladin en-Vec
Sanguine Guard
Searing Spear Askari
Shadow Rider
Soltari Crusader
Soltari Lancer
Southern Paladin
Suq'Ata Lancer
Sworn Defender
Teferi's Honor Guard
Varchild's Crusader
Warrior en-Kor
Western Paladin
White Knight
Youthful Knight
Zhalfirin Commander
Zhalfirin Crusader
Zhalfirin Knight

Knights
Knights of Thorn
Lost Order of Jarkeld
Order of the White Shield
Stromgald Cabal

Kobolds
Crimson Kobolds
Crookshank Kobolds
Kobolds of Kher Keep

Kraken
Polar Kraken

Leeches
Land Leeches

Legend
Adun Oakenshield
Angus Mackenzie
Asmira, Holy Avenger
Autumn Willow
Axelrod Gunnarson
Ayesha Tanaka
Barktooth Warbeard
Baron Sengir
Barrin, Master Wizard
Bartel Runeaxe
Boris Devilboon
Chandler
Commander Greven il-Vec
Crovax The Cursed
Dakkon Blackblade
Daughter of Autumn
Eladamri, Lord of Leaves
Eron the Relentless
Ertai, Wizard Adept

DECKBUILDERS' INDEXES

Nameless Race
Nameless Race

Narwhal
Narwhal

Nature Spirit
Maro

Necrosavant
Necrosavant

Nekrataal
Nekrataal

Niall Silvain
Niall Silvain

Night Stalker
Breathstealer
Feral Shadow
Shimian Night Stalker
Urborg Panther

Nightmare
Nightmare

Noble
Faerie Noble

Nomad
Ghitu Fire-Eater
Ghitu Slinger

Nomads
Avalanche Riders
Desert Nomads

Nymphs
Shanodin Dryads

Ogre
Ghazbán Ogre
Gray Ogre
Hasran Ogress
Ogre Enforcer
Ogre Shaman
Reckless Ogre
Sawtooth Ogre

Ooze
Chaotic Goo
Mwonvuli Ooze
Primordial Ooze

Orc
Orcish Captain
Orcish Farmer
Orcish Librarian
Orcish Lumberjack
Orcish Spy
Orcish Veteran

Orcs
Brassclaw Orcs
Ironclaw Orcs
Orcish Artillery
Orcish Cannoneers
Orcish Conscripts

Orcish Mechanics
Orcish Settlers
Orcish Squatters

Orgg
Orgg

Ouphe
Brown Ouphe

Oyster
Giant Oyster

Paladin
Lim-Dûl's Paladin
Northern Paladin
Order of the Sacred Torch
Serra Paladin

Peacekeeper
Peacekeeper

Pegasus
Armored Pegasus
Mesa Pegasus
Pegasus Charger

People Of The Woods
People of the Woods

Phantasm
Phantasmal Fiend
Phantasmal Forces
Phantasmal Mount
Phantasmal Sphere
Phantom Monster

Phoenix
Bogardan Phoenix
Firestorm Phoenix
Shard Phoenix
Shivan Phoenix

Pigeons
Carrier Pigeons

Pikemen
Pikemen

Pirates
Kukemssa Pirates

Pixie Queen
Pixie Queen

Poltergeist
Xenic Poltergeist

Pony
Dwarven Pony

Preacher
Preacher

Priest
Clergy of the Holy Nimbus

Pyknite
Pyknite

Python
Python

Rag Man
Rag Man

Raiders
Erg Raiders

Ranger
Kelsinko Ranger

Rats
Bog Rats
Crypt Rats
Diseased Vermin
Pestilence Rats
Plague Rats
Rabid Rats
Rats of Rath
Razortooth Rats
Sewer Rats

Rhino
Charging Rhino

Rhinos
Crash of Rhinos

Riders
Elven Riders

Robbers
Grave Robbers

Roc
Crimson Roc
Roc of Kher Ridges

Rock Sled
Goblin Rock Sled

Sage
Sage of Lat-Nam

Salamander
Cinder Crawler
Flowstone Salamander
Pyric Salamander
Scalding Salamander

Satyr
Willow Satyr

Scavenger Folk
Scavenger Folk

Scorpion
Pit Scorpion

Scout
Mtenda Herder

Scouts
Femeref Scouts

Serpent
Benthic Behemoth
Kukemssa Serpent

Marjhan
Sandbar Serpent
Sea Monster
Sea Serpent
Tolarian Serpent

Shade
Fetid Horror
Frozen Shade
Hoar Shade
Looming Shade
Mire Shade

Shadow
Nether Shadow

Shapeshifter
Anthroplasm
Dracoplasm
Escaped Shapeshifter
Morphling
Unstable Shapeshifter
Volrath's Shapeshifter

Shark
Giant Shark

Ship
Ghost Ship
Merchant Ship
Pirate Ship

Ships
Reef Pirates

Shyft
Shyft

Sindbad
Sindbad

Singing Tree
Singing Tree

Sisters
Sisters of the Flame

Skeleton
Carrionette
Lim-Dûl's High Guard

Skeletons
Drudge Skeletons
Restless Dead
Skeleton Scavengers
Unworthy Dead

Sliver
Acidic Sliver
Armor Sliver
Barbed Sliver
Clot Sliver
Crystalline Sliver
Heart Sliver
Hibernation Sliver
Horned Sliver
Mindwhip Sliver
Mnemonic Sliver
Muscle Sliver

Sengir Vampire
Skyshroud Vampire

Viashino
Retromancer
Viashino Bey
Viashino Cutthroat
Viashino Heretic
Viashino Outrider
Viashino Runner
Viashino Sandscout
Viashino Sandstalker
Viashino Sandswimmer
Viashino Warrior
Viashino Weaponsmith

Villain
Spinal Villain

Viper
Marsh Viper

Vultures
Osai Vultures
Wake of Vultures

Walking Dead
Walking Dead

Wall
Blistering Barrier
Carnivorous Plant
Cemetery Gate
Cinder Wall
Dark Maze
Drift of the Dead
Floodgate
Fog Bank
Glacial Wall
Illusionary Wall
Mindbender Spores
Shimmering Barrier
Sunweb
Thunder Wall
Tinder Wall
Vodalian War Machine
Wall of Air
Wall of Blossoms
Wall of Bone
Wall of Brambles
Wall of Caltrops
Wall of Corpses
Wall of Diffusion
Wall of Dust
Wall of Earth
Wall of Essence
Wall of Fire
Wall of Heat
Wall of Ice
Wall of Kelp
Wall of Lava
Wall of Light
Wall of Nets
Wall of Opposition
Wall of Pine Needles
Wall of Putrid Flesh
Wall of Razors
Wall of Resistance

Wall of Roots
Wall of Shadows
Wall of Souls
Wall of Stone
Wall of Swords
Wall of Tears
Wall of Tombstones
Wall of Vapor
Wall of Water
Wall of Wonder
Wall of Wood
Whip Vine

War-Riders
Varchild's War-Riders

Warthog
Warthog

Whale
Great Whale
Killer Whale

Whippoorwill
Whippoorwill

Wight
Dread Wight

Wiitigo
Wiitigo

Wildcats
Uktabi Wildcats

Wildebeests
Stampeding Wildebeests

Will-O'-The-Wisp
Will-O'-The-Wisp

Witches
Cuombajj Witches

Wizard
Apprentice Wizard
Archivist
Armorer Guildmage
Balduvian Conjurer
Civic Guildmage
Coffin Queen
Daring Apprentice
Disruptive Student
Fireslinger
Granger Guildmage
Keeper of the Beasts
Keeper of the Dead
Keeper of the Flame
Keeper of the Light
Keeper of the Mind
Krovikan Elementalist
Krovikan Sorcerer
Mage il-Vec
Magus of the Unseen
Mundungu
Oracle en-Vec
Prodigal Sorcerer
Reckless Embermage

Shadow Guildmage
Shaper Guildmage
Soldevi Machinist
Soldevi Sage
Stern Proctor
Suq'Ata Firewalker
Thalakos Deceiver
Thalakos Dreamsower
Thalakos Seer
Tolarian Entrancer
Wizard Mentor
Zuran Enchanter

Wizards
Academy Researchers

Wolf
Heart Wolf
Lone Wolf
Wyluli Wolf

Wolverine
Grizzled Wolverine

Wolverine Pack
Wolverine Pack

Wolverines
Rabid Wolverines

Wolves
Arctic Wolves
Dire Wolves
Timber Wolves
Tundra Wolves

Wombat
Rabid Wombat

Worm
Mana Leech

Worms
Insidious Bookworms
Mole Worms

Wraith
Bog Wraith
Dirtwater Wraith

Wretched
The Wretched

Wurm
Argothian Wurm
Barbed-Back Wurm
Craw Wurm
Dirtcowl Wurm
Elder Land Wurm
Endless Wurm
Fallow Wurm
Harvest Wurm
Johtull Wurm
Jungle Wurm
Rootbreaker Wurm
Scaled Wurm
Scoria Wurm
Segmented Wurm

Spined Wurm
Warping Wurm
Water Wurm
Wild Wurm
Winding Wurm
Yavimaya Wurm

Wyvern
Cerulean Wyvern

Yeti
Karplusan Yeti
Mountain Yeti

Zombie
Barrow Ghoul
Bone Dancer
Cackling Fiend
Carnophage
Dauthi Ghoul
Gravebane Zombie
Gravedigger
Phyrexian Ghoul
Plaguebearer

Zombies
Balduvian Dead
Bog Raiders
Drowned
Gangrenous Zombies
Legions of Lim-Dûl
Lim-Dûl's Cohort
Rank and File
Scathe Zombies
Zombie Mob
Zombie Scavengers

HACKABLE (CARDS THAT MENTION A LAND TYPE BY NAME)

Black Cards
Blanket of Night
Blighted Shaman
Bog Raiders
Bog Wraith
Corrupt
Desolation
Dirtwater Wraith
Evil Presence
Funeral Charm
Gangrenous Zombies
Hecatomb
Horror of Horrors
Infernal Denizen
Infernal Harvest
Legions of Lim-Dûl
Leshrac's Rite
Lost Soul
Marsh Lurker
Mire Shade
Mold Demon
Moor Fiend
Nightmare
Odylic Wraith
Plague Beetle
Quagmire
Stench of Evil

Strands of Night
Swamp Mosquito
Tourach's Chant
Veldrane of Sengir
Witch Engine
Withering Wisps
Zombie Master

Blue Cards
Acid Rain
Benthic Behemoth
Coral Reef
Dandán
Devouring Deep
Elder Spawn
Fishliver Oil
Flash Flood
Flooded Shoreline
Floodgate
Giant Shark
Hammerhead Shark
High Tide
Island Fish Jasconius
Kukemssa Serpent
Leviathan
Lifetap
Lingering Mirage
Lord of Atlantis
Magical Hack
Manta Ray
Marjhan
Merchant Ship
Merfolk Assassin
Merfolk Raiders
Mind Bend
Mystic Decree
Part Water
Pirate Ship
Psychic Allergy
Reality Twist
River Merfolk
Sea Monster
Sea Serpent
Seasinger
Segovian Leviathan
Serendib Djinn
Snowfall
Tidal Warrior
Undertow
Veiled Serpent
Viscerid Drone
Vodalian Knights
Volcanic Eruption
Water Wurm
Waterspout Djinn

Green Cards
Anaconda
Aspect of Wolf
Bayou Dragonfly
Blanchwood Armor
Bull Elephant
Bull Hippo
Carpet of Flowers
Cat Warriors
Choke
Deadfall
Dire Wolves

Eladamri, Lord of Leaves
Elven Palisade
Erhnam Djinn
Foratog
Fortitude
Fungus Elemental
Gaea's Bounty
Gaea's Liege
Gaea's Touch
Gargantuan Gorilla
Gorilla Pack
Heartwood Giant
Heartwood Treefolk
Hidden Path
Living Lands
Llanowar Druid
Mirri, Cat Warrior
Nature's Lore
Nature's Wrath
Pale Bears
People of the Woods
Pygmy Allosaurus
Quirion Ranger
Rime Dryad
River Boa
Rogue Elephant
Roots of Life
Rootwater Alligator
Scarwood Bandits
Scarwood Hag
Shanodin Dryads
Spreading Algae
Thelon's Chant
Thelonite Druid
Thelonite Monk
Thoughtleech
Treefolk Seedlings
Tsunami
Typhoon
Uktabi Wildcats
Unseen Walker
Vernal Bloom
Village Elder
Waiting in the Weeds
Warthog
Weatherseed Elf
Wood Elemental
Wood Elves
Wormwood Treefolk

Red Cards
Active Volcano
Blood Moon
Boil
Burrowing
Canyon Wildcat
Cave People
Chaos Moon
Crevasse
Curse of Marit Lage
Dwarven Pony
Dwarven Sea Clan
Enslaved Scout
Eternal Flame
Fireblast
Flashfires
Glacial Crevasses
Goblin Caves

Goblin Flotilla
Goblin King
Goblin Rock Sled
Goblin Scouts
Goblin Shrine
Goblin Ski Patrol
Goblin Spelunkers
Goblins of the Flarg
Granite Grip
Kird Ape
Mountain Goat
Mountain Yeti
Omen of Fire
Orcish Farmer
Orcish Lumberjack
Quarum Trench Gnomes
Raiding Party
Rathi Dragon
Reign of Chaos
Scald
Sedge Troll
Spitting Earth
Vug Lizard

White Cards
Angry Mob
Aysen Highway
Celestial Dawn
Conversion
Drought
Femeref Scouts
Great Wall
Island Sanctuary
Karma
Lifeblood
Righteous Avengers
Royal Decree
Spiritual Sanctuary
Tithe

Artifact Cards
Cyclopean Tomb
Gauntlet of Might
Kormus Bell
Naked Singularity
Sandals of Abdallah
War Barge

Gold Cards
Acidic Sliver
Adun Oakenshield
Altar of Bone
Angus Mackenzie
Arcades Sabboth
Army Ants
Asmira, Holy Avenger
Axelrod Gunnarson
Ayesha Tanaka
Barktooth Warbeard
Bartel Runeaxe
Benthic Djinn
Boris Devilboon
Breathstealer's Crypt
Cadaverous Bloom
Centaur Archer
Chromatic Armor
Chromium
Circle of Despair

Corrosion
Crystalline Sliver
Dakkon Blackblade
Dark Heart of the Wood
Delirium
Diabolic Vision
Discordant Spirit
Dracoplasm
Earthlink
Elemental Augury
Emberwilde Caliph
Energy Arc
Energy Bolt
Essence Vortex
Femeref Enchantress
Fiery Justice
Fire Covenant
Firestorm Hellkite
Flooded Woodlands
Frenetic Efreet
Fumarole
Gabriel Angelfire
Ghostly Flame
Giant Trap Door Spider
Glaciers
Gosta Dirk
Grim Feast
Guiding Spirit
Gwendlyn Di Corci
Halfdane
Harbor Guardian
Haunting Apparition
Hazerider Drake
Hazezon Tamar
Hibernation Sliver
Hunding Gjornersen
Hymn of Rebirth
Jacques le Vert
Jasmine Boreal
Jedit Ojanen
Jerrard of the Closed Fist
Johan
Jungle Troll
Kaervek's Purge
Kasimir the Lone Wolf
Kei Takahashi
Kjeldoran Frostbeast
Lady Caleria
Lady Evangela
Lady Orca
Leering Gargoyle
Lim-Dûl's Paladin
Lim-Dûl's Vault
Livonya Silone
Lobotomy
Lord Magnus
Lord of Tresserhorn
Malignant Growth
Marhault Elsdragon
Marsh Goblins
Merieke Ri Berit
Misfortune
Monsoon
Mountain Titan
Mundungu
Nature's Blessing
Nebuchadnezzar
Nicol Bolas

Titania's Chosen
Tropical Storm
Undergrowth
Verdant Force
Waiting in the Weeds
Whirling Dervish
Willow Priestess

Red Cards
Active Volcano
Anarchy
Battle Frenzy
Beasts of Bogardan
Burnout
Chaos Moon
Chaoslace
Cinder Cloud
Crimson Hellkite
Defender of Chaos
Disorder
Dwarven Song
Evaporate
Fork
Goblin Offensive
Goblin Scouts
Goblin Soothsayer
Goblin Warrens
Goblin Wizard
Guma
Havoc
Heat Wave
Keeper of Kookus
Lightning Cloud
Magnetic Mountain
Mogg Infestation
Mountain Yeti
Omen of Fire
Orcish Healer
Orcish Lumberjack
Orcish Veteran
Parch
Pyroblast
Pyrokinesis
Raiding Party
Red Elemental Blast
Reign of Chaos
Rukh Egg
Sirocco
Spinal Villain
Subterranean Spirit
Sulfuric Vapors
Tooth and Claw
Varchild's War-Riders
Wildfire Emissary

Blue Cards
Abjure
Balduvian Shaman
Blue Elemental Blast
Breath of Dreams
Cerulean Wyvern
Chill
Coral Reef
Douse
Dreams of the Dead
Elder Spawn
Ether Well
Flash Flood

Force of Will
Fylamarid
Hibernation
Homarid Shaman
Homarid Spawning Bed
Hydroblast
Insight
King Crab
Krovikan Sorcerer
Manta Ray
Merchant Scroll
Mind Harness
Narwhal
Ovinomancer
Phantasmal Sphere
Riptide
Sea King's Blessing
Sea Sprite
Sea Troll
Sleight of Mind
Spiny Starfish
Suffocation
Sunken City
Suq'Ata Firewalker
Thoughtlace
Tidal Control
Tidal Influence
Tidal Wave
Wall of Kelp
Weatherseed Faeries
Word of Undoing
Wrath of Marit Lage

Black Cards
Abomination
Bad Moon
Balduvian Dead
Barbed-Back Wurm
Bereavement
Black Carriage
Black Knight
Breach
Breeding Pit
Broken Visage
Burnt Offering
Carrion
Cemetery Gate
Commander Greven il-Vec
Contagion
Corrupting Licid
Crypt Rats
Cursed Flesh
Dark Banishing
Darkest Hour
Dauthi Horror
Deathgrip
Deathlace
Derelor
Dread of Night
Drudge Spell
Dystopia
Eastern Paladin
Ebony Charm
Eviscerator
Fear
Feast or Famine
Ghost Hounds
Gloom
Grave Servitude

Hellfire
Horror of Horrors
Ihsan's Shade
Inquisition
Irini Sengir
Jovial Evil
Kaervek's Hex
Knight of Stromgald
Lab Rats
Leshrac's Sigil
Marsh Lurker
Minion of Leshrac
Nameless Race
Nocturnal Raid
Norritt
Order of Yawgmoth
Order of the Ebon Hand
Perish
Phyrexian Boon
Priest of Yawgmoth
Purraj of Urborg
Rank and File
Razortooth Rats
Reign of Terror
Ritual of the Machine
Sacrifice
Sarcomancy
Sengir Autocrat
Sleeper's Guile
Soldevi Adnate
Soul Rend
Spinning Darkness
Spirit of the Night
Stromgald Cabal
Stronghold Taskmaster
Suq'Ata Assassin
Terror
Thrull Wizard
Tombstone Stairwell
Touch of Darkness
Wall of Putrid Flesh
Western Paladin
Yawgmoth's Edict

NON-STANDARD LANDS THAT PRODUCE
OR USE MANA OF A CERTAIN COLOR

Black
Badlands
Bayou
Bottomless Vault
Castle Sengir
Cinder Marsh
Ebon Stronghold
Everglades
Koskun Keep
Lake of the Dead
Lava Tubes
Pine Barrens
Polluted Mire
River Delta
Rootwater Depths
Salt Flats
Scrubland
Sulfurous Springs
Underground River
Underground Sea
Urborg
Wizards' School

Blue
Adarkar Wastes
Aysen Abbey
Caldera Lake
Castle Sengir
Coral Atoll
Land Cap
Remote Isle
River Delta
Rootwater Depths
Sand Silos
Skyshroud Forest
Svyelunite Temple
Thalakos Lowlands
Tolaria
Tolarian Academy
Tropical Island
Tundra
Underground River
Underground Sea
Volcanic Island
Wizards' School

Green
An-Havva Township
Aysen Abbey
Bayou
Brushland
Gaea's Cradle
Havenwood Battleground
Heart of Yavimaya
Hollow Trees
Jungle Basin
Karplusan Forest
Koskun Keep
Mogg Hollows
Pendelhaven
Pine Barrens
Savannah
Skyshroud Forest
Slippery Karst
Taiga
Timberline Ridge
Tropical Island
Vec Townships
Veldt

Red
An-Havva Township
Badlands
Caldera Lake
Castle Sengir
Cinder Marsh
Dormant Volcano
Dwarven Hold
Dwarven Ruins
Hammerheim
Karplusan Forest
Koskun Keep
Lava Tubes
Mogg Hollows
Plateau
Scabland
Smoldering Crater
Sulfurous Springs
Taiga
Timberline Ridge
Volcanic Island

DECKBUILDERS' INDEXES

White
Adarkar Wastes
An-Havva Township
Aysen Abbey
Brushland
Drifting Meadow
Icatian Store
Karakas
Karoo
Kjeldoran Outpost
Land Cap
Plateau
Ruins of Trokair
Salt Flats
Savannah
Scabland
Scrubland
Serra's Sanctum
Thalakos Lowlands
Tundra
Vec Townships
Veldt
Wizards' School

NON STANDARD LANDS THAT DO NOT PRODUCE OR USE MANA OF ANY PARTICULAR COLOR (INCLUDES LANDS THAT CAN PRODUCE MANA OF ANY COLOR)

Adventurers' Guildhouse
Ancient Tomb
Arena
Bad River
Balduvian Trading Post
Bazaar of Baghdad
Blasted Landscape
Cathedral of Serra
City of Brass
City of Shadows
City of Traitors
Crystal Vein
Desert
Diamond Valley
Elephant Graveyard
Faerie Conclave
Flood Plain
Forbidding Watchtower
Gemstone Mine
Ghitu Encampment
Ghost Town
Glacial Chasm
Grasslands
Griffin Canyon
Halls of Mist
Ice Floe
Island of Wak-Wak
Library of Alexandria
Lotus Vale
Maze of Ith
Maze of Shadows
Mishra's Factory
Mishra's Workshop
Mountain Stronghold
Mountain Valley
Oasis
Phyrexian Tower
Quicksand
Rainbow Vale

Reflecting Pool
Rocky Tar Pit
Safe Haven
School of the Unseen
Scorched Ruins
Seafarers' Quay
Sheltered Valley
Shivan Gorge
Soldevi Excavations
Sorrow's Path
Spawning Pool
Stalking Stones
Strip Mine
Teferi's Isle
Thawing Glaciers
The Tabernacle at Pendrell+
Thran Quarry
Treetop Village
Undiscovered Paradise
Unholy Citadel
Urza's Mine
Urza's Power Plant
Urza's Tower
Volrath's Stronghold
Wasteland
Winding Canyons

NON-STANDARD LANDS THAT LET YOU FETCH ANOTHER LAND AND PUT IT INTO PLAY

Bad River
Flood Plain
Grasslands
Mountain Valley
Rocky Tar Pit
Thawing Glaciers

CARDS WITH CYCLING

Artifact Cards
Fluctuator

Enchantment Cards
Lingering Mirage
Power Taint
Rune of Protection: Artifa+
Rune of Protection: Black
Rune of Protection: Blue
Rune of Protection: Green
Rune of Protection: Lands
Rune of Protection: Red
Rune of Protection: White
Sicken
Veiled Serpent

Instant Cards
Brand
Clear
Expunge
Iron Will
Lull
Radiant's Judgment
Rebuild
Repopulate
Rescind
Scrap
Swat

Interrupt Cards
Miscalculation

Land Cards
Blasted Landscape
Drifting Meadow
Polluted Mire
Remote Isle
Slippery Karst
Smoldering Crater

Sorcery Cards
Hush
Rejuvenate
Lay Waste
Unearth

Creature Cards
Bloated Toad
Cloud of Faeries
Darkwatch Elves
Disciple of Grace
Disciple of Law
Drifting Djinn
Pendrell Drake
Sandbar Merfolk
Sandbar Serpent
Shimmering Barrier
Wild Dogs

CARDS THAT PREVENT DAMAGE OR ALLOW DAMAGE TO BE PREVENTED

Artifact Cards
Al-abara's Carpet
Amulet of Kroog
Balm of Restoration
Bone Mask
Conservator
Dark Sphere
Pentagram of the Ages
Rakalite
Shield of the Ages
Squee's Toy

Enchantment Cards
Alms
Circle of Despair
CoP: Artifacts
CoP: Black
CoP: Blue
CoP: Green
CoP: Red
CoP: Shadow
CoP: White
Energy Field
Errant Minion
Fylgja
Greater Realm of Preservation
Hidden Retreat
Hot Springs
Lim-Dûl's Hex
Martyr's Cause
Penance
Power Leak
Prismatic Circle
Righteous Aura
Rune of Protection: Artifact
Rune of Protection: Black

Rune of Protection: Blue
Rune of Protection: Green
Rune of Protection: Lands
Rune of Protection: Red
Rune of Protection: White
Samite Blessing
Serra's Hymn
Soul Barrier
Thought Lash

Instant Cards
Alabaster Potion
Anoint
Bandage
Desperate Gambit
Guardian Angel
Heal
Healing Salve
Honorable Passage
Invulnerability
Ivory Charm
Redeem
Remedy
Sacred Boon
Scars of the Veteran
Shadowbane
Temper

Land Cards
Oasis

Sorcery Cards
Mind Bomb
Stench of Evil
Torrent of Lava

Summon Cards
Ali from Cairo
Argivian Blacksmith
Balduvian Hydra
Clergy en-Vec
Combat Medic
Elvish Healer
Ethereal Champion
Femeref Healer
Kei Takahashi
Mercenaries
Nafs Asp
Orim, Samite Healer
Sabertooth Cobra
Samite Alchemist
Samite Healer
Sanctum Custodian
Sanctum Guardian
Seasoned Tactician
Serra Paladin
Soldevi Heretic

CARDS WHICH ALLOW THE PLAYER TO GAIN OR STEAL LIFE

Artifact Cards
Balm of Restoration
Bottle Gnomes
Claws of Gix
Crystal Rod
Delif's Cone
Elixir of Vitality
Essence Bottle
Fountain of Youth

Blue
Bazaar of Wonders
Field of Dreams
In the Eye of Chaos
Mystic Decree
Teferi's Realm

Green
Arboria
Concordant Crossroads
Hall of Gemstone
Living Plane
Revelation

Red
Caverns of Despair
Chaosphere
Elkin Lair
Gravity Sphere
Land's Edge
Storm World

White
Eye of Singularity
Null Chamber
Serra Aviary

Gold
Winter's Night

ENCHANT CREATURE CARDS

Black
Binding Agony
Casting of Bones
Cloak of Confusion
Coils of the Medusa
Cursed Flesh
Dark Privilege
Death Watch
Demonic Torment
Despondency
Endless Scream
Enfeeblement
Fear
Feast of the Unicorn
Funeral March
Grave Servitude
Imprison
Krovikan Fetish
Krovikan Plague
Leshrac's Rite
Mind Whip
Paralyze
Parasitic Bond
Phyrexian Boon
Sadistic Glee
Seizures
Sicken
Sleeper's Guile
Soul Kiss
Spinal Graft
Spirit Shackle
Takklemaggot
Thrull Retainer
Torment
Torture
Treacherous Link
Unholy Strength

Vampiric Embrace
Vampirism
Weakness

Blue
Abduction
Anti-Magic Aura
Apathy
Awesome Presence
Backfire
Betrayal
Binding Grasp
Cloak of Invisibility
Cloak of Mists
Contempt
Control Magic
Creature Bond
Cunning
Curiosity
Dream Coat
Errant Minion
Essence Flare
False Demise
Fishliver Oil
Flight
Gaseous Form
Hermetic Study
Invisibility
Launch
Mana Chains
Merseine
Mind Harness
Mystic Veil
Pendrell Flux
Phantom Wings
Puppet Master
Robe of Mirrors
Shimmering Wings
Slow Motion
Snow Devil
Soar
Spectral Cloak
Tangle Kelp
Thirst
Unstable Mutation
Vanishing
Venarian Gold
Viscerid Armor
Volrath's Curse
Zephid's Embrace

Green
Armor of Thorns
Aspect of Wolf
Bequeathal
Blanchwood Armor
Briar Shield
Carapace
Cocoon
Decomposition
Fortitude
Frog Tongue
Gaea's Embrace
Gift of the Woods
Instill Energy
Lure
Maddening Wind
Mammoth Harness
Mortal Wound

Nature's Chosen
Nature's Kiss
Predatory Hunger
Rancor
Regeneration
Roots
Snowblind
Spider Climb
Venom
Venomous Fangs
Wanderlust
Web

Red
Aggression
Agility
Bestial Fury
Betrothed of Fire
Brand of Ill Omen
Bravado
Burrowing
Consuming Ferocity
Crown of Flames
Destructive Urge
Dizzying Gaze
Earthbind
Errantry
Eternal Warrior
Fiery Mantle
Fire Whip
Firebreathing
Flowstone Blade
Giant Strength
Granite Grip
Immolation
Imposing Visage
Ironclaw Curse
Lightning Reflexes
Maniacal Rage
Mob Mentality
Paroxysm
Reflexes
Shiv's Embrace
Sluggishness
Stonehands
Tahngarth's Rage
The Brute
Veteran's Voice

White
Armor of Faith
Artifact Ward
Black Scarab
Black Ward
Blessing
Blue Scarab
Blue Ward
Brainwash
Brilliant Halo
Cessation
Conviction
Cooperation
Divine Transformation
Empyrial Armor
Farrel's Mantle
Favorable Destiny
Flickering Ward
Fylgja
Green Scarab

Green Ward
Hero's Resolve
Holy Armor
Holy Strength
Infinite Authority
Kithkin Armor
Kjeldoran Pride
Lance
Pacifism
Pariah
Prismatic Ward
Red Scarab
Red Ward
Ritual of Steel
Samite Blessing
Seeker
Serra Bestiary
Serra's Embrace
Shackles
Spirit Link
Sun Clasp
Ward of Lights
White Scarab
White Ward

Gold
Chromatic Armor
Spectral Shield
Wings of Aesthir

INTERRUPTS

Black
Burnt Offering
Dark Ritual
Deathlace
Sacrifice
Songs of the Damned
Spoils of Evil
Withering Boon

Blue
Abjure
Annul
Arcane Denial
Blue Elemental Blast
Counterspell
Deflection
Desertion
Dismiss
Disrupt
Dissipate
Ertai's Meddling
Flash Counter
Forbid
Force Spike
Force Void
Force of Will
Hydroblast
Interdict
Intervene
Magical Hack
Mana Drain
Mana Leak
Meddle
Memory Lapse
Miscalculation
Power Sink
Rebound

DECKBUILDERS' INDEXES

DECKBUILDERS' INDEXES

Forbidden Ritual
Fugue
Gaze of Pain
Haunting Misery
Hellfire
Hymn to Tourach
Icequake
Ill-Gotten Gains
Infernal Contract
Infernal Harvest
Inquisition
Jovial Evil
Kaervek's Hex
Lab Rats
Living Death
Mind Peel
Mind Ravel
Mind Twist
Mind Warp
Nausea
Ostracize
Painful Memories
Perish
Persecute
Phyrexian Tribute
Pox
Rain of Tears
Raise Dead
Reanimate
Reign of Terror
Reprocess
Ritual of the Machine
Shattered Crypt
Sinkhole
Soul Burn
Soul Exchange
Spoils of War
Stench of Evil
Stupor
Syphon Soul
Tendrils of Despair
Touch of Death
Unearth
Unnerve
Victimize
Word of Binding
Yawgmoth's Will

Blue
Æther Tide
Acid Rain
Amnesia
Ancestral Memories
Argivian Restoration
Baki's Curse
Braingeyser
Diminishing Returns
Drafna's Restoration
Drain Power
Dream Cache
Energy Tap
Exhaustion
Fade Away
Flux
Foresight
Forget
Juxtapose
Legerdemain
Library of Lat-Nam
Mana Severance

Merchant Scroll
Mind Bomb
Paradigm Shift
Part Water
Political Trickery
Polymorph
Portent
Prosperity
Psychic Purge
Psychic Transfer
Ransack
Recall
Reconstruction
Relearn
Show and Tell
Sift
Theft of Dreams
Tidal Surge
Time Ebb
Time Spiral
Time Walk
Time Warp
Timetwister
Tinker
Transmute Artifact
Undo
Volcanic Eruption
Windfall

Green
An-Havva Inn
Channel
Creeping Mold
Desert Twister
Elven Cache
Elven Rite
Essence Filter
Eureka
Fallow Earth
Forgotten Lore
Gaea's Blessing
Gaea's Bounty
Hurricane
Hush
Ice Storm
Metamorphosis
Mulch
Natural Balance
Natural Order
Natural Spring
Nature's Lore
Nature's Resurgence
Needle Storm
Overrun
Rampant Growth
Rebirth
Regrowth
Rejuvenate
Renewal
Seeds of Innocence
Stream of Life
Stunted Growth
Summer Bloom
Superior Numbers
Taste of Paradise
Thermokarst
Titania's Boon
Tranquility
Tropical Storm
Tsunami

Typhoon
Untamed Wilds
Unyaro Bee Sting
Verdant Touch
Waiting in the Weeds
Whirlwind
Wing Snare
Winter Blast
Winter's Grasp

Red
Acidic Soil
Aftershock
Anarchy
Apocalypse
Arc Lightning
Avalanche
Builder's Bane
Chain Lightning
Cone of Flame
Deadshot
Detonate
Disintegrate
Disorder
Earthquake
Eternal Flame
Evaporate
Falling Star
Fanning the Flames
Fireball
Fit of Rage
Flame Wave
Flashfires
Flowstone Flood
Gamble
Game of Chaos
Goblin Grenade
Goblin Offensive
Goblin Scouts
Hammer of Bogardan
Illicit Auction
Jagged Lightning
Jokulhaups
Kaervek's Torch
Lava Axe
Lava Burst
Lay Waste
Mana Clash
Meltdown
Meteor Shower
Mob Justice
Mogg Infestation
Pillage
Primitive Justice
Pyroclasm
Pyrotechnics
Rain of Salt
Raze
Reign of Chaos
Relentless Assault
Retribution
Rolling Thunder
Ruination
Scorched Earth
Seething Anger
Shadowstorm
Shatterstorm
Song of Blood
Spitting Earth
Steam Blast

Stone Rain
Torrent of Lava
Tremor
Wheel of Fortune
Wildfire
Winds of Change
Winter Sky

White
Angelic Blessing
Armageddon
Balance
Blinding Light
Cataclysm
Catastrophe
Cleanse
Cleansing
Dust to Dust
Gerrard's Wisdom
Icatian Town
Leeches
Martyr's Cry
Path of Peace
Peace Talks
Pegasus Stampede
Planar Birth
Prophecy
Purify
Repentance
Resurrection
Retribution of the Meek
Shahrazad
Tariff
Tivadar's Crusade
Visions
Winds of Rath
Wrath of God

Gold
Altar of Bone
Diabolic Vision
Energy Bolt
Fiery Justice
Fumarole
Hymn of Rebirth
Kaervek's Purge
Lobotomy
Misfortune
Phyrexian Purge
Savage Twister
Sealed Fate

INDEX

MAKE ROOM.

The *Magic: The Gathering*® –*Mercadian Masques*™ expansion brings on Mercenary and Rebel cards that will redefine the horde; get one on the table, then root through your deck for others every turn.

Tired of that four-card limit? With the new Spellshapers you can turn any card in your hand into a timely spell like Unsummon or Stone Rain. It's like topdecking the card you need, any time.

The set also introduces premium basic lands— now you can create all-premium decks.

Mercadian Masques. Instant gratification.

Mercadian Masques

Questions? (800) 324-6496

www.wizards.com

ANY PORT IN A STORM

Far from the maelstrom of Rath, the *Weatherlight* comes to rest near the mysterious city of Mercadia. Here the crew grieve for fallen comrades and attempt to repair the ravaged vessel. But they must do so quickly. For in Mercadia, everything has a price.

And they may soon pay with their lives.

The *Mercadian Masques* novel ties directly to the **Magic: The Gathering**®— *Mercadian Masques*™ expansion. Get the story behind the cards and experience the adventure only hinted at in flavor text.

Look for it at better book and hobby stores everywhere.

September 1999

www.wizards.com